Praise for Stephen Knight's writing:

'...re is a level, heart-breaking voice from the outskirts of Larkin country, grow... bbier, quirkier, more garish and desolate, but for all that, inde... ble.' Joseph Brodsky

'Ste... n Knight is a poet who juxtaposes the surreal with the banal to sh... ow one is the strange cousin of the other ... his is an urban wo... lgy and strangely lit, at its most vivid when described in the ech... ull rhyme that he handles so well.' Helen Dunmore, *Observer*

'... *City Cinema* is urban, allusive, seriously jokey, formally dashing. ... book is full of newness; it's very exciting in itself, and for what it ... is Stephen Knight might do next.' Andrew Motion

Mr Schnitzel

STEPHEN KNIGHT

VIKING

VIKING

Published by the Penguin Group
Penguin Books Ltd, 27 Wrights Lane, London w8 5tz, England
Penguin Putnam Inc., 375 Hudson Street, New York, New York 10014, USA
Penguin Books Australia Ltd, Ringwood, Victoria, Australia
Penguin Books Canada Ltd, 10 Alcorn Avenue, Toronto, Ontario, Canada m4v 3b2
Penguin Books (NZ) Ltd, Private Bag 102902 NSMC, Auckland, New Zealand

Penguin Books Ltd, Registered Offices: Harmondsworth, Middlesex, England

First published 2000
1 3 5 7 9 10 8 6 4 2

Set in 15.5/18.5 pt Monotype Centaur
Typeset by Rowland Phototypesetting Ltd, Bury St Edmunds, Suffolk
Printed in Great Britain by Clays Ltd, St Ives plc

A CIP catalogue record for this book is available from the British Library

ISBN 0−670−88832−x

for my parents

Just because his life is often bewildering to him, the child needs even more to be given the chance to understand himself in this complex world with which he must learn to cope. To be able to do so, the child must be helped to make some coherent sense out of the turmoil of his feelings. He needs ideas on how to bring his inner house into order, and on that basis be able to create order in his life . . .

The child finds this kind of meaning through fairy tales.

Bruno Bettelheim, *The Uses of Enchantment*

Acknowledgements

With thanks to Karl Knight and Roland Hafen-richter for inspiring a couple of the footnotes, and to Alexandra Pringle and Kate Goodwin for their encouragement and support.

Contents

PREFACE

In 1967, aged four, I spied a pair of winkle-pickers on a fellow bus-passenger. My demand, bellowed to my mother and, inadvertently, the entire lower-deck — 'I WANT A PAIR OF POINTY SHOES BEFORE I DIE' — passed into family lore. It was joined, in time, by the ferry incident (a gregarious seven-year-old, I regaled travellers on the Dover–Calais crossing with jokes and songs for much of the journey) and the moment in Austria when I was tricked into swimming.

The trouble is, I don't know if I remember the bus and ferry episodes or if I'm recalling my parents' versions of events. Similarly, transcribing these seven bedtime stories, I couldn't be sure which elements originated with my father and which I had added over the years. In the end, I was inclined to think it didn't matter, that recording them was enough. My twenty-six footnotes, however, are another matter.

If I'm honest, I rarely bothered with footnotes in the past — their whiff of pedantry, the way they interrupt the narrative, the little typeface. So you can imagine my surprise when they began to grow from the bottom of the page, rising up, until they became as important an act of retrieval as the tales themselves. Now, I read every note that comes my way.

I.

HERMANN

Before the Wright Brothers, before Blériot, before Alcock and Brown but after the Montgolfier Brothers, there was Able Seaman Hermann, the fabulous and now forgotten Birdman of the Austrian Navy.

Hermann discovered the marvellous properties of his breath one day shortly after joining the service in the middle of the nineteenth century. A Tuesday. He had drunk too much schnapps, as cadets do, and was returning to his barracks on the outskirts of Salzburg, on tiptoe over the gravel for fear of waking the guard.

'*Halt!* Who *ist das?*' the sentry shouted into the dark.

This startled Hermann. He threw both arms in the air and pleaded for clemency, which in turn startled the sentry, who had only been practising anyway.

'Hermann?' he said, when the figure of the half-cut cadet emerged from the gloom. 'Is that you?'

[My father only knew a few words of German so he had to revert to English whenever his characters spoke to one another at any length or used words he could never remember.]

Ill-coordinated, Hermann came to a halt much too

close to the sentry, a superior officer who caught the smell of alcohol at once.

'Have you been drinking?' the sentry demanded, leaning in close to Hermann. 'In the town, perhaps? At Bertha's[1] Guest-House?'

'*Nein, mein Herr,*' said a swaying Hermann.

Upsettingly for our hero, the sentry had two bristly moustaches balanced on two sets of full lips below two pairs of eyes that drilled into Hermann. Hermann groaned involuntarily.

'Stand to attention!' the sentry bellowed.

Hermann did as he was ordered, though he couldn't

---

1. This was one of my father's nicknames for my mother. He would initiate me into his rebellion with a wink, then, a tiny smile at the corner of his mouth, continue with the story. Bertha was probably from the big gun the Germans used in the Great War. Other nicknames included Brünnhilde, Blossom, Ethel (a 1970s coinage, after a character in the novelty record 'The Streak', with its phrase *Too late, Ethel!*), the Führer, Hectic Heli, Minnie, Schultz or Schultzy, Thora and Fred. Fred was a legacy of the big freeze of 1963, when my parents re-concreted our cracked driveway and my mother worked as hard as my father, mixing cement six months before I was born. A titan, she dwarfed my little father. The nickname derives from 'Right, Said Fred', another novelty song, this one about a bunch of idle builders. (It was commemorated in a pair of egg-cups labelled *Eduard* and *Fred* in Gothic lettering.)

He continued to call her one or more of these names even after she had lost everything and gone mad.

stop rocking as if buffeted by a high wind. The sentry completed a circuit of him, as sentries do, looking him up and down, seeking the label that said THIS MAN IS DRUNK. He stopped in front of Hermann and faced him, nose-tip to nose-tip. The smell of booze was obvious but he had to make sure.

'Pre-zent BREATH!' he barked.

Hermann, wobbling, opened his mouth then aahhed at the superior officer. The stink was so powerful that the sentry, who was that rarity among Austrians, a confirmed teetotaller, was forced to step back. The gust of breath caught the peak of the sentry's cap and lifted it off his head and several centimetres into the air.

'Aaahhhhhhh.'

The man was stunned. He couldn't believe what had happened. Able Seaman Hermann's pickled breath had lifted his cap into the air. How could that be possible? It was against the Laws of Nature, against all rational thought, and the sentry was nothing if not rational. You need look no further than the perfectly trimmed nostril hairs, the pores on his face purged of all blackheads and the extreme neatness of his pair of moustaches to understand that. He stood aghast for a moment, and then his training took over.

'Pre-zent BREATH!' he shouted, this time holding his cap in the line of fire.

'Aaahhhhhhh.'

Sure enough, it rose like a balloon. There was no

mistaking it. Here was the proof. The Able Seaman had helium breath.

Well, the sentry corrected himself pedantically, breath with the properties of helium.

The news spread at an alarming pace, first through the barracks and the sentry's superiors, then throughout Naval Command in Vienna, on to the royal household then out to the inns and backstreets of Vienna and from there, in a matter of years — this being the age of the horse — to the rest of the Austro-Hungarian Empire. Hermann was a miracle, a wonder of the modern age, and, best of all, he was the Emperor's.

The Emperor of the time, by common consent a silly man, had thoughts of showing off his prize to the crowned heads of Europe, his uncles, aunts and cousins, as a *By Royal Appointment* freak, one better than a jester or juggler, though the Admiralty soon persuaded His Majesty that Hermann was of greater value as a secret weapon. Momentarily peeved that his toy was being taken away from him, the Emperor agreed to a period of research and development with Hermann's peculiar talent. So it was that Hermann went from anonymous Able Seaman to the Navy's worst-kept secret weapon. In the inns and the guest-houses the talk was all of Hermann and his amazing talent even though, as a precautionary measure, the Emperor had forbidden journalistic reporting of this phenomenon. Instead, Hermann's fame passed from household to household by word of mouth, exaggerated in the telling each time until Hermann's lungs were attributed with the power to raise elephants, regiments, even buildings, into the air. This hearsay suited the Emperor, who was of a mind to frighten his enemies abroad, and what better way than with rumours of an extraordinary warrior.

In the meantime, boffins with wild white hair and distracted expressions were set the task of making full use of Hermann's talents. They came up with the idea of using him as a one-man self-inflating spy balloonist. Launched from a warship when the wind was in the right direction, Hermann would sail over the enemy's fleet, reporting back their strength and position by means of semaphore. In early tests, Hermann's enthusiastic flag-flapping moved him out of position as well as making him a highly visible target for enemy marksmen.

'*Schnell*, Hermann. Another circuit of the Palace!' his coach shouted every day, as a leaner, fitter Hermann was put through his paces.

'I'm doing my best,' was Hermann's catch-phrase as he staggered past the square-jawed petty officer.

A record of his progress was kept by a favourite of the Emperor, a vague man who had taken to the newfangled art form of photography.[2] His task was to capture Hermann in the various stages of his preparation:

2. Before he switched to model railways, my father was a keen amateur photographer, so this is probably a self-portrait. When

7

a. Before training sessions (dry-vested).
b. After training sessions (damp-vested).
c. On the ground, with shrivelled pigs' bladders at ankles, waist and shoulders.
d. Airborne, holding his flags aloft in the service of the Emperor.

This photographer, whose name has been more thoroughly forgotten than even the exploits of Hermann, was also charged with keeping a diary of the Birdman's triumphs and set-backs, though the Emperor would, no doubt, have suppressed the latter.

---

his enthusiasm faded over the years – 'I'm too old to bother with all that' – he relegated to the attic his boxes and carousels of slides, the battered screen he pulled down like a blind, the projector (its beam of dusty light more exciting than the slides themselves), scuffed ring-binders fat with strips of negatives in greaseproof-papery sleeves to protect them from scratching, bottles of smelly chemicals and the jars into which they were decanted, the home-made red light (with a towel tucked under the door, our kitchen doubled as a darkroom: my mother was told to keep out for a couple of hours; a crack of light could ruin everything), the clock I used to operate – 'Now,' he would say crisply for me to start it, then a slurred 'Ssssstop' as he kept the negative exposed to the paper for another tenth of a second – the trays I rocked like a cradle, watching the developer lapping the edges, washing over the shiny paper as, supernaturally – shadows first, eye sockets, hair, lips, nose – the picture appeared. The products of all this paraphernalia

A lazy man enthused by cameras, the photographer continually postponed the diaries to another day, scribbling notes on receipts for shirts or bills from guest-houses, then stuffing them into a trunk in his room at the Palace. The receipts mounted up but the notebook supplied for the journal remained blank, the rough pages uncut, the cover unmarked.

On the day of the great disaster, Hermann had trained as usual, twenty laps of the Palace grounds, his breath visible in the autumn air, his feet crunching on the gravel like a little boy eating cornflakes. When, panting, he posed for yet another photograph, his breath was captured on

---

were shoved into anything with a lid, hundreds of black-and-white prints my mother nagged him to label before there was no one left to remember who the people were and when they were alive. Austria alone must have filled a suitcase: the mountains, the guest-houses, my mother's relatives snapped over thirty years. I would offer to sit down with the two of them and plough through the archive but we never did get around to it, even though I went as far as buying sticky labels for the job one Christmas Eve. The only occasion we ever sifted through photographs together was in my mother's home town, Knittelfeld, during our last holiday together and the only time I've been there as an adult.

We were invited to dinner by my Aunt Christl, who had divorced Helmut, the youngest of my three uncles, after twenty years of a marriage entered into because she was pregnant with their first daughter. As far as I could tell, it was an amicable split born out of boredom rather than infidelity, and Christl

film like ectoplasm emerging from a medium's lips. He changed for what was to be the final demonstration of his skill, wearing heavy brocade in honour of the Emperor and Empress, who were throwing another party to show off their man. Hermann was to ascend from a platform in the middle of the vast, ornamental lake at the heart of the Palace grounds and then, from a hundred feet up, signal his devotion to the Emperor.

Bedecked in the shrivelled bladders, he bowed equally low to the royal party, the hangers-on, the bodyguards and the truly great.

'Your Highnesses, my Lords, *meine Damen und Herren* . . .'

---

continued to keep in touch with us, sending postcards from Greece or the Austrian lakes (Britain was never a holiday destination) and telephoning at New Year and on birthdays. For my mother, twenty years her senior, Christl was the sister she never had, a source of comfort when things began falling to pieces, someone she could talk to in German.

Christl still lived in Knittelfeld, not far from her ex-husband, on the edge of town, where new houses in varying stages of completion inched skyward. The builders were young couples who had bought land on which to build their dream. Everyone chipped in to help these dreams along, though the usual scene was a lone man and a wheelbarrow moving between piles of sand, a cement mixer chewing at one end of the site. Impatient young families moved in before the plaster was on the walls.

Christl overlooked these beginnings from her own new beginning, a compact third-floor flat, its living room and dining area combined. Dough figures of a farmer and his wife hung

(Hermann's etiquette lessons proved their worth that chilly afternoon in the Palace grounds) 'I will now demonstrate the power I am happy to pledge to the Emperor. Your servant.'

At this point, Hermann bowed again. Despite his polish, his poise and his brocade, he bore a worrying resemblance to Stan Laurel; his long face, his hair in shock. Unflustered by the occasion, he took into his mouth the tube that would inflate the bladders and began blowing like a piper. Gradually the balloons began to expand, creaking quietly as they did. The observant among the assembled nobility might have noticed Hermann's

---

on the wall, beside the steel-and-glass drinks cabinet where we were welcomed with tall glasses of Campari and orange juice that glowed like flames. At the far end of the room, no more than a dozen paces from the table, the lace-curtained window opened on to a balcony and another block of flats rising from the long grass, the future taking shape. In the distance, a blue mountain darkened in the early evening.

We arrived to discover a black smudge on the ceiling, the lampshade singed, and a red plastic spatula melted like a Dali clock, the only evidence of an accident with the fondue set that had ruined my aunt's preparations moments earlier. It took a while for my mother to coax a panda-eyed Christl out of her bedroom. She had wanted everything to be perfect for her special guests. We were there to meet Ernst, a jolly Gendarm in flip-flops that showed off chubby baby's toes. His gelled hair bounced forward irrepressibly whenever he laughed, which was often that night, beginning as he handed

plimsolled feet touching the ground a little less firmly with each passing second.

They *might* have noticed but didn't, because they were too busy tucking into champagne and canapés provided by the Royal Chefs marching to and from the Royal Kitchens in a wobbly-hatted procession that moved fluidly around the tables like a conga line. Slowly, Hermann rose. The shadow that was stretching from his toes was now beneath the soles of his feet. A centimetre became two inches, two inches became a foot, a foot became six feet, six feet became sixty [my father always mixed metric with

---

us our Camparis then attempted conversation with no more than a dozen words of English. The same build, the same round faces, the same broad smiles, he and Christl could have been brother and sister. I glimpsed my mother through the open door, sitting on the bed next to a sniffing Christl, her arm lying on my aunt's shoulder like a yoke. A fluffy polar bear and a doll were slumped on the snowy coverlet, leaning squiffily against the headboard. It was the room of a girl on the edge of puberty.

When they eventually emerged – Christl freshly made up, new eyes and a shade of lipstick that didn't really suit her – fondue was abandoned for grilled chunks of meat. The evening continued as though the fire had never happened, my mother translating the more convoluted bits of the conversation to keep things going, turning from Ernst and Christl (who spoke a little English) then back to my father and me like a tennis umpire, translating selectively, putting her own spin on discussions that ranged from the cost of dentistry to Bosnian

imperial measurements], and still Hermann puffed for all he was worth. Blasé and over-fed, the entourage managed a drip-drip of applause that barely carried one hundred feet up into the air where the bladders and Hermann were swelling together, the former with air, the latter with pride. The frilled and perfumed wives, in many cases fatter than their fat husbands, fidgeted generously upholstered bottoms in generously upholstered seats, crashing back against them like whales. Limp-handed applause was no reward for all the hard work the Birdman and his trainer had put into the exhibition, not to mention

---

refugees. From time to time, Ernst placed his hand on Christl's to attract her attention, asking if he should fetch another bottle of wine or telling her that the food was tasty.

'Christl,' my father said, leaning forward after dessert, his rheumy eyes twinkling, a smile flickering at the edge of his mouth, giveaways that he thought he was about to be amusing, 'in four years . . . I will be married to Helma for . . . fifty years,' – the 'fifty' emphasized with mock-astonishment – 'and I . . . will have . . . *eine* . . . GOLD . . . MEDAL . . . for being married . . . to a Mödritscher . . .'

Coming from anyone else, Christl might have taken it as a dig at her failed marriage, but this was Mister Schnitzel (an honorary title bestowed on my father by Uncle Hari, the middle brother, in recognition of the meal my father ate at least four times a week while in Knittelfeld). Married to an Austrian for nearly half a century without ever learning German, even though my parents had holidayed in Austria every year since the late sixties, he communicated by smiling, talking slowly

the bravery Hermann exhibited being up so high without a parachute.

[As far as my father knew, and Da Vinci notwithstanding, the parachute was a device some years in the future.]

Even from where he was, Hermann noticed that his reception was not as enthusiastic as he had expected. Despite the months of rehearsal, the rigorous hours of

---

and clowning. With no subtlety of expression available to him, he was obliged to play the fool, a role he took to with an uncomplicated pleasure. Far from being frustrated by his inability to join in with the gossip, he seemed content to lapse into momentary silences, only to return with an observation prompted by a phrase my mother had decided to translate – her commentary was not only unreliable but intermittent – or with a belated response to a subject that had gone around the table half an hour earlier. My relatives must have found his contribution to gatherings more than a little surreal, like the delays in a satellite link-up between astronauts and their loved ones back on earth. During our holidays, my mother sank into her first language, luxuriating in her role as intermediary, the glue in any get-together, the one who came to know all the tittle-tattle, which she dispensed to the monoglots. This was probably just as well, because she couldn't bear to be left out of anything. Everyone's business was her business. If it hadn't been for our bedtime stories of the Austrian Navy, my father's speech for the four weeks there would have stuck on monosyllables and might have dwindled into aphasia.

'*Eine*. . . GOLD. . . MEDAL,' he repeated, as though the translation of the indefinite article would make all the difference for Christl and Ernst.

work with his glowing-biceped petty officer, the lessons in manners from a well-meaning but dull Professor from Berne, Hermann decided to attract the crowd's attention. He did not, of course, consider what he was about to do mere showmanship. No, for Hermann it was an aerial display, the first of its kind as far as anybody knew, a demonstration of his manoeuvrability and daring.

My mother waved her hands at him in mock annoyance. By now we were tipsy, our consonants wrapped in cotton wool. After second helpings of blackberry tart, Christl produced the first of four dark-glassed bottles of Sekt and, from the bedroom, two shoeboxes and a padded album. One by one, she set photographs reverentially on the table while Ernst finished a story no one but my mother had followed, though even she had listened with one eye on the bottle as it was set down on the table then opened, the cork squeaking satisfactorily as it was released from its glass girdle. The photographs were curved like the bottom of a boat.

Christl spoke to me in her best English. 'They are from your Oma and Opa.'

Oma and Opa: my Austrian grandparents. After the disposal of cheap ornaments, dresses, suits and shoes, brooms, buckets, and the gadget that clipped over the television screen to magnify the picture, and after the sharing out of tables and chairs, cutlery and the working electrical appliances, no one but Christl had wanted the photographs. Most of the older prints were no bigger than their negatives – the figures tiny and unrecognizable – others had serrated edges and sepia shadows. They were exotically different from our own back home. My mother's grandparents were stern-faced and frozen

'A-N-D N-O-W,' he flapped with his coloured flags, 'F-O-R M-Y N-E-X-T T-R-I-C-K . . .'

It was a phrase he had heard at the circus. Although aware that it might demean what he was about to do, he couldn't think of anything better. Then he blew a little more of his magic breath into the pigs' bladders to break

---

for the long exposure and there were photographs going back to the First World War, my grandfather at seventeen in uniform puttees, a bayonet at his side, holding an alpenstock that was taller than he was, posing against the painted backdrop of a snow-capped mountain. His companion, broader but looking as young, stood beside him, making my grandfather look even smaller, but ready none the less to face my father's father and uncles across no-man's land. On seeing this particular portrait, my mother leaned over to me.

'I bet if I ask for this, Christl will say say no,' she said in a stage whisper.

Christl's response – the tone said 'Of course,' though I couldn't tell you exactly what was said – surprised my mother, though I didn't understand why she thought Christl would deny her an eighty-year-old photograph of her own father. She held the print in her two hands, looked at it for a moment without speaking, then slipped it into her handbag (between her driving licence and her calorie-counter booklet), the perfume of receipts, tissues, groschen, lipstick, and salvaged postage stamps wafting from soft pockets.

The oldest photograph dated from the turn of the century – my great-grandparents locked in family groupings, scarcely daring to breathe – the most recent from the mid sixties, my father's snaps of my brother and me swimming, playing in the

his own altitude record, a cherry on the cake of the death-defying feats he was about to present.

Alas, poor Hermann hadn't noticed the icicles braiding his bladders nor the velvety frost on his blond and sepia uniform. On the C in TRICK, one of Hermann's flags launched an icicle into a balloon on his left shoulder at

---

garden or on the beach, sent by my mother to her parents, her best handwriting on the back. There were photographs too of my grandfather in the Second World War. Imprisoned in the 1930s for being a communist, he was conscripted into the German occupying force in France, even though he was in his mid forties.

'I remember my father being taken away when I was a girl,' my mother said. 'In the middle of the night. I held on to him. I must have been six or seven. Because he was a communist they wouldn't give him work.'

My grandfather looked shrunken in his ill-fitting grey uniform, his eyes overshadowed by the helmet. Too old to fight, he served with a detail assigned to locate and identify the unmarked graves of soldiers, covering ground that had been fought over only weeks before. I watched my mother's face, looking for a change, wondering how many glasses of wine she had drunk and wishing I had counted. As I watched her huge hands cradling the photographs one by one, Ernst refilled her glass and she took a sip unthinkingly. When I looked up, I could see that he and Christl were watching us with a quiet pride, their smiles blurred by the wine.

Out of the blue, 'I remember my grandfather's funeral passing when I was three,' my father announced. 'I was with Auntie Gertie, in the street. She turned me away to face a shop window.

the same time as one at his waist popped with a dull thud. The loss of a bladder was catered for in the design of Hermann's flying machine although, that morning, Hermann had over-indulged at breakfast and was a

---

The blinds were down and I could see the reflection of the plumed horses and the men following the hearse.'

Then, as if he hadn't spoken a word, he passed me a photograph of his in-laws as a young couple standing with their bicycles, my grandmother in a dirndl, a scarf wrapped like a turban around her head, my grandfather with his heavy moustache, grown out when he'd realized the earlier version made him look like Hitler. Günther, my mother's eldest brother, sat astride the crossbar of his father's bicycle, his bare legs dangling at least a foot off the ground, his toes pointed like a ballet dancer's. He couldn't have been more than four.

'Look, Stefan,' Christl said. 'Your mother.'

Christl handed me one of a series of photographs charting my mother's early years. In the first, she was standing alone in a field in the late 1930s, her pigtails down to her waist, un-embarrassed, looking the camera in the eye. Almost in sequence, the years were passed around the table. My mother in her teenage years at the end of the war, posing coquettishly with Günther beside a tree. My grandparents, older now, with Hari at their side and Helmut in Oma's arms. Then photographs of my parents as newly-weds, her nineteen and him twenty-eight, dispatches from Wales sent to my grandparents in lieu of a visit.

'My father wanted me back home,' my mother said, looking at a photograph of her wedding. 'I broke his heart.'

'Oh, here she goes again. Moaning Minnie,' my father mut-

fraction heavier than he ought to have been. In matters of science, every ounce is important one way or another and an extra slice of garlic sausage could mean the difference between success and failure.

———————

tered. 'Your mother has never been able to make a decision in her life. That's what you have to realize.'

My father took the photograph of their wedding from me and studied it blankly. Between his thumb and forefinger there was a dark bruise the colour of the blackberry juice smeared on our plates. A cut self-inflicted the day before, it looked as though it would never heal. 'That's what age does,' he said when I asked him why it looked so angry.

Eager to participate, Ernst handed me another photograph. 'You,' he said.

Aged five, I was sulking in a trilby, my big ears perched on the side of my head like butterflies. My mother took the portrait from me and it was tiny in her great palms.

'I wish I was young again,' she said.

'Let's have a look at diddums,' my father said to wind me up, dispelling the maudlin atmosphere like a magician releasing doves.

I wondered what he thought, seeing fragments of his own past laid out on the table, pictures of his own parents in among Christl's collection. There were no names written on the back. When they are handed down from Christl to her children and then her grandchildren, no one will know who they are. They wouldn't even recognize my father in these photos tracing his journey from smiling youth to smiling middle-age, his hair thinning, his mouth filled with that too-good-to-be-true evenness of dentures, his eyebrows wilder with every year that passed.

'I don't know how you two ever got together,' I said.

'I W-I-L-L . . .'

Hermann's signalling was interrupted by a sudden lurch as the slow puncture of the shoulder-bladder gaped. Alarmed but with his wits about him, Hermann began to inflate the spare bladder while continuing to signal to the indifferent throng below.

'I W-I-L-L P-E-R-F-O-R-M A M-A-N-O . . .'

Hermann struggled with the spelling of *manoeuvre*, flapping madly like a pheasant surprised by beaters.

[At this point my father would ask me if I could spell the word to help Hermann but, aged six, I could not. In class, we were only at the beginning of our bright red spelling-book, but I had peeked at the back, where unpronounceable words like *Egypt* and *yacht* were lying in wait. *Manoeuvre* was a long way off.]

Hermann's embarrassed flapping was exacerbated by his inability to inflate the bladders fully, having used most of his puff on the morning run. His eyes were wide with surprise.

If anyone had been able to hear, '*Mein Gott*' might have been Hermann's last words.

Even my mother, with reason to be maudlin, laughed at pictures of Günther looking like Errol Flynn or me as a baby sitting on my brother's lap, my legs splayed like a frog's.

It was after midnight and the last bottle of Sekt was empty. Despite Christl's protestations, nobody at the table could finish the final piece of tart left in its dish among the drifts of photographs.

It all happened in a flash, so quickly that the photographer, whose moustache was greasy with sausage fat, failed to capture Hermann's final seconds in the air. Both flags pierced bladders at the same time as, in shock, Hermann allowed the breath from the spare bladder to rush back into his mouth, dizzying him.

Phhhhhhhhhhh.

That, and the ice that had formed on all parts of his body, brought him plunging to earth like a fridge. One or two of the retinue gasped, several thought it the trick Hermann had only half-announced, but most were too busy quaffing their fourth glass of champagne or munching their umpteenth *bratwurst* on a stick to notice Hermann leaving the sky so unceremoniously, hitting the water of the ornamental lake with a fountained splash before sinking to the bottom. Juggling his camera and tripod in one hand and a flute of bubbly and a cucumber sandwich in the other, the photographer managed to reach the water's edge in time to capture concentric circles breaking soundlessly on the mossy edge of the lake.

There, in the middle of that liquid target, a single bladder bobbed on the surface.

The Emperor was present for Hermann's send-off, the Royal Tear-Maker at his side ministering to His Majesty's utterly unaffected ducts.

A stone was erected outside Salzburg. Beneath a royal eagle with its wings stretched to their full span was the simple inscription:

ABLE SEAMAN HERMANN

BIRD MAN

though this monument vanished without trace one night at the end of the Second World War, carried away by the Red Army to who knows where.

On the first anniversary of Hermann's accident, an exhibition of the photographer's work was held in the Royal Gallery. It was a small affair – the Emperor didn't want the entire world to know of the failure – and when one courtier noted that a few portraits seemed to be on the pale side no one paid attention. On the second anniversary, at the insistence of the petty officer, who had grown fond of Hermann even as he had been bawling at him, the exhibition was mounted again, though no one noticed that there were fewer pictures on the wall, nor that many appeared to have been taken in a snowstorm, fading like upholstery left in the sunlight.[3] The solid

3. One year, I must have been six or seven, I persuaded my parents to take a stack of my comics on holiday with us. Perhaps they were a security blanket, perhaps I was terrified of being engulfed by all that German, on menus, on signs, from the mouths of the men and women whose gold teeth caught the

squares of Hermann's uniform were turning to winter breath, his fair hair whitening. It wasn't until a week into the second exhibition that people began to comment on the blanched squares hanging on the wall. Questions began to be asked and an article appeared in a prominent newspaper which mentioned the phenomenon in the course of a debate about photography as an art form. Despite rumours, however, and one journalist's momentary interest in the case, the photographer could not be traced. He had faded from sight as completely as the details in his photographs. All that was found, among the unwashed dishes in the sink, the heap of smelly socks strewn on the floor, and the wrinkly sheets of the unmade bed in his lodging house on the outskirts of Vienna, was a trunkful of receipts covered with his scribbles, every

---

light when they bent to pat the top of my head. Even Hoss and Little Joe spoke German. In the boot of the car, the comics travelled everywhere with us, wedged in by towels, a football, toys and bulging suitcases. I remember looking in there at Klopeinersee and noticing those comics, untouched all the time we were there, as flat as when they were new. The sun must have somehow got to work on them, or else the acid left in the paper after the printing process reacted with the fresh air of Austria. Years later, when I rediscovered them while rooting around in the loft, I found the cover of the comic on top of the pile faded to a shadow of its former, full-colour glory. A drawing of Neil Armstrong planting the Stars and Stripes on the lunar landscape, it was bleached to a ghost.

item of his photographic equipment, and a note in a typically careless scrawl that said:

I couldn't master fixatives.

[When I asked my father how he knew about Hermann, he turned to a large, padlocked chest in a corner of my grandparents' bedroom, and grinned.]

2.

THE BARON

'The Austrians were at war with Spain, so the mighty Baron . . .' my father began, and I closed my eyes to listen carefully to what he had to say, anticipating an explanation for his absence.[4]

4. Stories for a five-year-old unsettled by sleeping in a strange bed in a strange country, the tales of the Austrian Navy began on the second visit to my mother's real home. There were so many, repeated so often with so many variations and cross-fertilizations of details that, by the time I had heard my last story, they had formed one mighty saga of heroism on the High Seas and in the Gulf of Austria.

In a way, they began because my parents couldn't afford a holiday together in the first years of their marriage. Before I was born, my mother crossed the continent by train with my older brother in tow while my father stayed at home and worked through the summer. She would be gone for weeks. They had no telephone in the fifties so communication was limited to letters, though my mother was never much of a letter-writer, a fact I put down less to a shakiness with her second language than the size of her fingers: a biro was a matchstick in her hand, a sheet of Basildon Bond a postage stamp. If there were Christmas cards to sign or forms to fill in, it was always my father's handwriting that appeared for both of them. One time at Swansea station, so the family legend goes, my father walked

The Baron was introduced sulking in his igloo on top of one of the highest mountains in Austria while his countrymen struggled against the Spaniards at balmy sea-level. A cold man by nature, the Baron had taken to his ice-house in a fit of pique, after the woman he was to marry fled the country with a leather-jacketed Duke in tow. His ridiculously large, walrus moustache bristled like

_____

straight past my mother on the platform. With a brand-new coat and a few extra pounds of weight, she wasn't the woman he'd waved off weeks before. Given her height, I doubted this, but my father never let facts spoil a good story.

'Good God, what's happened to you?!' he asked, and she replied in German.

'*Guten Tag*,' my three-year-old brother said, when my father bent down to greet him.

I first visited Austria as a baby. We didn't go as a family until 1968, when I was five, and even then the journey was staggered. My mother, who could take a long holiday from her job spraying toy cars and humping boxes in Louis Marx, went on ahead with me while my father, who couldn't wangle as much time off from the steel works where he was an accounts clerk, set off at least a week later, driving across the continent in our first car, a sky-blue Austin 1100. My teenage brother was the navigator. I'm told I missed my father on the train and in the days before he joined us, demanding to know where he was. When he finally arrived in the middle of the night, making up for his absence with the first tale told sitting on the billowy duvet that engulfed me like a wave, I lay wide awake, staring at him in amazement, my feet nowhere near the bottom of the bed.

a forest fire when he heard the news and, frozen inside, he vowed to grow icicles from it as an outward sign of his hardened heart. This was a common event in Imperial Austria and would have gone unnoticed by the Three Estates were it not for the fact that the Baron was both an infamous duellist and a formidable military strategist who had earned the respect of all Austrians in his encounters with Napoleon's fleet. His ploys, it was whispered, drew on the manifold laws and mysteries of accountancy.

He had been brooding in his igloo on the Dachstein for a year when word came of the war with Spain via the blue hands of an underdressed messenger from the Emperor.

'Go away,' the Baron said, on hearing a knock on his freezing door.

Chunks of snow broke away from his home as the messenger continued rapping on it.

'B-B-Baron,' the messenger shivered, '*eine* muh-muh-message from the Cuh-Court.'

'Very well,' the Baron boomed, his voice threatening an avalanche. '*Aber mach schnell.*'

Throwing the snowy door wide, the Baron faced the frozen messenger, his puny body buckled under the weight of the cold, his teeth chattering *Ich bin kalt* in Morse code, his feet encased in blocks of ice. Inside, the Baron could make out the messenger's fat toes poking from his shoes. When this once ebullient man tried to read from the brittle, Imperial scroll his words shook, consonants and vowels shearing away to plunge into the gorge below.

'GIVE IT TO ME, OAF!'

Icebergs calved in Antarctica. Snatching the message from the trembling hands — snapping off a few words of salutation and praise in the process — the Baron scanned the parchment, noting the Emperor's seal and signature at the bottom. Although it was wreathed in the diction and syntax of absolute authority, the message was clearly a plea for help. It began with an appraisal of the war between Spain and Austria (the threatened borders, the Imperial Army's heavy defeat, the Navy in disarray), then continued with lavish praise for the Baron, his great victories, his wisdom, his valour — praise that the Baron found himself reading aloud to the messenger thawing out under seventeen blankets.

'"... *your battles with the savages of Southern Europe and your conquests of the Seven Seas are talked about with such delight at Court we scarce know where to end our cataloguing* ..." Praise indeed,' the Baron said, and an icicle fell from his huge moustache. 'I will return with you.'

Flattery had done the trick and the Baron, casting aside the days of his frozen heart, donned another layer of furs, strapped tennis racquets to his feet, picked up his sword and headed for the valley, the messenger following at a stagger, wrapped in the seventeen blankets, sinking to his chest in powdery snow.

News of the Baron's return travelled fast, and within a week the courtiers were talking of nothing else.

'*Der weiße Riese* is coming! *Der weiße Riese* is coming!'[5]

Expectation moved around the palace; murmurs, whispers, nodding heads, the sigh of a lady-in-waiting drifting down a shadowy corridor like the smell of bread. Vienna swept its cobbled streets and laid red carpet wherever it was thought the Baron's feet might tread. Banners were unfurled from flagpoles, and the Baron's coat of arms (a sword, an abacus, a furry hat and snow-tigers rampant), copied and displayed in the windows of countless residences throughout the city, soon became the only doodle on schoolchildren's exercise books. Even the most pompous civic dignitaries, grateful for an opportunity to wear their chains of office, dug out old medals from the corners of cupboards and the backs of drawers as proof that they too were once heroes, half wishing they could join the Baron in his adventure with the villainous Spaniards.

Two days of preparation took the city to a degree of excitement normally reserved for coronations, visits of foreign royalty and the first snow. Now, the Baron was as good as royal. Had the Empire not been in need of his great strategic brain, the Emperor might have regarded

5. *Weiße Riese* (White Giant) was a washing powder advertised on television during our earliest holidays. An Austrian housewife, her hands at either side of her mouth like a megaphone, bellowed *WEIßE RIESE!* into the snow-capped mountains. *Mit riesen Waschkraft* said the authoritative, male voice-over.

him as a threat, a candidate for banishment if not imprisonment. As it was, when the Baron appeared at the far end of a long red carpet in the Palace, still wrapped in furs, the Emperor considered racing towards the dot in the distance and embracing it, though, in the end, he restricted himself to a little wave that the Baron returned after a moment, initially reluctant to compromise his dignity. The lines of armour-plated, lance-bearing sentinels flanking the carpet did not flinch.

'CLEMENT WEATHER, BARON,' the Emperor bellowed.

'INDEED, YOUR MAJESTY. I HAD NOT THOUGHT TO FEEL A SUN So Warm again,' the Baron shouted.

Bowing low as he spoke, his final words were lost in the thick pile of the carpet. This was the Baron's second concession to royalty. The first, devoting half a day to trimming his unruly moustache, left him looking like Rhett Butler.[6]

After a full minute of walking at a stately pace, they met in the middle of that massive room where the Baron

6. This was the detail that told me the Baron was based on my Uncle Günther. Older and taller if not broader than my mother, Günther was the only man who could talk her into silence, tell her what to eat and drink, lead her through a house she knew already and make her listen to his commentary. He loomed in the dark corners of my earliest holidays like a dragon, rumbling, unpredictable, liable to erupt; and he was full of

bowed again. Less deeply this time, the Emperor could not fail to notice.

'Baron,' the Emperor said.

'Your Majesty,' the Baron said.

'So good of you to return.'

The Baron said: 'Yes.'

The Emperor said: 'Spain.'

The Baron said: 'Indeed.'

The pair then began to talk in a whisper unheard by even the nearest of the highly polished guards flanking the strawberry-red carpet, whispers speculated about by generations of historians, whispers that will for ever remain a mystery.

[Even my father didn't know.]

Within an hour, the course of action was determined and, bowing once more, the Baron embarked on his long journey to the end of the carpet, through the Palace courtyards smelling of horses, and on to the Austrian Fleet and glory, a scroll of the finest parchment in his nerveless hand, a star-shaped medal pinned to his furry chest.

---

secrets. He had fought for the Germans in World War Two, though he was never a Nazi. He had blown up a tank with a bazooka. Even my mother didn't know for sure if her brother really had spent the final months of the war in the SS, a conscripted student sent to face the Russians. She knew he had served in the Army (the story was it helped to keep my grandfather out of a concentration camp), but Günther's

The voyage to confront the Spanish Armada was an arduous one, days of tempestuous winds with waves like the faces of ugly cliffs, then nights of eerie stillness and a ghostly moon, though the men were buoyed up by the presence of the Baron on deck, facing the gale that failed to ruffle his Brylcreemed hair and his neat moustache, or standing apart in the dark, contemplative but stern, his new medal gleaming in the moonlight. He was, the sailors recognized, as heroic as standard-issue knickerbockers allowed. (Normally a flamboyant dresser, the Baron had thought it only right that he should wear what the other officers wore, a gesture appreciated by the junior ratings on every vessel of the mighty Austrian Fleet.)

It was on one of those eerie nights, when the crews were obliged to row their four-masted ships with extremely

---

particular misfortune was that his height qualified him, so my brother believed, for the SS. When the Russians entered Berlin, he abandoned his uniform in the basement of a burnt-out building then walked to Vienna – Cottbus, Reichenburg, Snezka, Brünn in Czechoslovakia, Retz and Zellendorf – a journey of thirty days, dodging cossacks who chased him and his companions into a bog in a wood near Dresden. Only the horses sinking in the quagmire saved them. Up to his chest in shitty water, holding his breath, shivering, he was as quiet as a ghost until the soldiers rode away. For me, it was impossible to think of him hiding, a hunted man afraid of death.

He posed for the only photograph I ever took of him on the final day of that last visit to Austria, on my way to the station,

long-handled oars, that the Spanish threat appeared on the horizon like an ominous cloud. Through his spyglass, the Baron could make out the glinting guns bristling from stem to stern of every battleship.

'Prepare for an engagement, Sir?' an eager officer enquired when he saw the Baron put the telescope to his left eye. 'The men will follow you to the ends of the earth.'

'Stand by,' the Baron drawled.

[For some reason, my father always used to impersonate John Wayne at this point. I never questioned the logic.]

As one, the crew of every ship of the Austrian Fleet held its breath, looking to the masts of the flagship and waiting for the signal 'A-U-S-T-R-I-A

---

ragged clouds blotting out the mountain tops like cannon smoke, rain hammering down, pouring off the neighbouring roofs and filling holes in the building site opposite, September a couple of days away. Prompted by my mother, I fished my camera out of my case while a more than usually agitated Günther, after trying a pose at the window and another at the door to his office, strode to the desk where he still worked, even though he had long since retired. There were more circulars and postcards than business letters and window envelopes scattered over the wide pampas of the desk. Arms folded, he sat behind his electric typewriter, his Anglepoise leaning in subserviently, his blue telephone perched on a metal arm that held it above the desk like a piece of dental equipment, three ash-coloured in-trays stacked inside one another, and a hunting rifle hanging from its strap on the wall behind him, below

E-X-P-E-C-T-S . . .' that would soon hang limply over-head. It did not come.

'Signal the Fleet to follow us!' the Baron barked, splin-tering the northern silence. 'Bo'sun. Redouble the rowing. *Schnell!* Set a new course, Helmsman.'

The puzzled crew followed orders in a daze, their bewilderment increasing when they realized that their course took them closer to the Spaniards then away in a wide arc, as though making a feint, as though enacting a change of mind.

'We're running away,' one old tar murmured to another,

---

a line of four certificates, each with my uncle's name in copper-plate. Kundl, his 'lady friend' (my father's term), stood at his back, a hand on either shoulder as though she were stopping him from exploding like a jack-in-the-box. His boyish legs visible under the desk, he was in good shape for a man past seventy, though, his tanned face melting with wrinkles, he was as mortal as the interlinked, grey, bevelled squares of the sixties wallpaper. It might have been a more impressive portrait if he had bothered to change out of his pyjama top.

A moneyed, middle-class museum, his house stood on its own in a field throughout my childhood, aloof, undisturbed by neighbours. It was easy to believe the surrounding land was his, even though there was a low wall around the house and gardens. I always thought it proper that someone so successful should live as my uncle did. Not only did a vast acreage befit his status (he sold insurance), but it was clear that a good deal of space was needed to quarter his tempestuousness. One of the rituals of our summers in Austria was a conducted tour of

and the word spread like fire from crow's nest to poop deck to galleys and bilges. 'We're running away.'

'The heading is north,' the Baron shouted.

With little wind to assist them, the sailors were forced to man the oars, which they did with a great deal of cursing and disgruntlement.

The indignity! The loss of honour! To assist in an act of cowardice!

This was in the days when a drummer at the prow beat out the stroke, a steady rhythm for a steady progress. The Baron, mindful of the sense of urgency required of

---

Günther's property, the annual event when he showed off his latest purchases: a food mixer, a colour television, a dishwasher, a garage with an automatic door, satellite channels. I realized only years later that this must have tormented my mother, who left an Austria broken by the war, thinking she would be better off in Britain. Whenever I imagine the Austria of that time it is the Vienna of *The Third Man* (the grey rubble Joseph Cotten picked his way through to track down Orson Welles, the shadows, the defeated people), so I didn't find it at all surprising she had left. That my mother had travelled from Austria with a zither, the instrument responsible for the famous theme tune of Carol Reed's film, only strengthened the connection. Like everything else, it finished up in our attic, unplayed, with only a few strings unbroken. My mother tried a tune on it once, but the sound was discordant and the strings hurt her fingertips.

'Eddie. *Schau!*' Günther would command, sweeping his arm like a ringmaster to reveal his television's twenty-inch screen.

his fleet, sent orders down to quicken the pace, and no sooner had the oarsmen settled down to a less-than-punishing rate than the rhythm-keeper was drumming like Ringo Starr on an especially fast Beatles number, 'She Loves You' or 'I Saw Her Standing There'. Aghast at what was asked of them, doubting the strategy, the oarsmen nevertheless kept pace with the frantic thumping. The Austrian Fleet cut through the water like a shark. In the

---

'*Sehr gut*, yes,' my father replied, looking down at the television then up to my towering uncle. '*Ein gut*... picture, *jawohl*?' He nudged me. 'I bet you'd like one of those, eh?' Then back to Günther with 'Stefan . . . *hat* . . . square eyeballs!'

(Sure enough, a few years later, when the money had been saved, a television like my Austrian uncle's was next to me on the back seat of our car, driven home from town to save on the cost of delivery. We knelt together for hours, my father and me, puzzling over the instructions spread on the floor among the plastic and the polystyrene shapes, my mother stamping in and out, tutting, saying we should have paid the extra to have it installed by experts.)

While my father admired Günther's set he was oblivious to my mother's growing agitation, her lips thinning, the air forced in and out of her nostrils. I could hear her snorting breath and knew there would be trouble if a door wasn't opened and the tendrils of her annoyance released.

'You told my parents I would only be working for a few years.'

My mother's voice, choked by an undergrowth of anger, came out like a whiny, small bird's cheeping.

'Here we go again.' My father turned to his brother-in-law and shook his head, sighing, 'Helma.'

distance, on watch aboard one of the Spanish ships, a keen-eared Able Seaman heard a far-off, excitable heart-beat getting louder by the minute. Peering into the darkness he could see a black shape, a mountain rearing from the waves, Atlantis rising, or the sea itself on its hind legs.

'*Capitano! Capitano!*' the nervous Spaniard called, waking his sleeping compatriots. 'It is the enemy.'

He was looking for support, a nod or a smile that might bridge the linguistic divide, like a soldier crossing no-man's land on Christmas Day, an indication that Günther, by then divorced, understood marriage, the toll it took, the compromises. Adjusting the picture on his television, boosting the brightness until the people on the screen were lost in a mist, then demonstrating just how loud the volume could go, my uncle had no idea what was going on. I plugged my ears with my fingers.

Reminders of my mother's wrong turning in life continued throughout my adolescence and into adulthood, the bad years when, to escape the arguments and recriminations, the tantrums and threats, the flying crockery, I no longer travelled across Europe with them. Her telephone calls to me were full of indignation, booze, and snide remarks about her brother's latest slave. Even my name was a mistake, so, at her prompting, I was called Stefan by the Austrian side of the family. When, years older and nearly as tall as Günther, I did go back, the tour was still on his timetable.

'Take your shoes off inside,' my mother said.

We were standing on the long, covered porch outside two doors at right-angles to one another. One door led straight to the office while the other opened into the hall.

By the time the sailors of the Spanish Fleet were roused, the shape on the horizon had become the Austrian Fleet, ensigns crackling on masts, oars striking the water furiously, and what little wind there was pushing out the sails like a stomach swollen by over-eating. Spanish cannons were wheeled into position, powder monkeys darted among their elders with supplies, the officers waxed their

---

'Jesus! What have you got in here, the crown jewels?' My father struggled with my case.

'Nothing,' I muttered, trying not to look shifty as I relieved him of the weight.

'It's a wonder the aeroplane got off the ground, carrying this lot.'

I had told my parents about the flight when they'd met me at Vienna airport; the orange upholstery of the seats faded to the sepia of old photographs, the crackly airline anthem sung to the tune of Rod Stewart's 'Sailing':

> *You are welcome*
> *You are welcome*
> *Austrian Airlines*
> *Welcomes you . . .*

'It's just a few bits and pieces.'

I took the case from him and staggered into the hall. Inside, I could see that the three of us had changed more than the building, which showed its age in matters of style rather than decay. Our stockinged feet touched the chilly tiles.

'Günther!' my mother called. 'Günther! GÜNTHER!'

I was remembering the block floor, its dark burgundy and purple squares, the whorls of the wooden banister, even a

moustaches in preparation for Death or Glory, and the man way up in the crow's nest put away his knitting and looked skyward to pray to the Lord for deliverance.

[Despite his atheism, my father always included details like this. Come to think of it, I'm surprised his communism didn't prevent his use of the aristocracy as heroic figures altogether. I suppose he wasn't one to indoctrinate.]

---

mirror, in the same place after twenty years, when a tanned woman in her mid seventies emerged from the kitchen, wiping her hands on a tea towel, her eyes downcast momentarily as though she felt she ought not to have been there.

'*Servus*,' my mother said, continued in a German dialect too quick to follow, then finished with 'This is Kunigunde,' when I was no longer looking.

'Kundl,' Kunigunde said.

We shook hands mutely, the two of us nodding like fools, our smiles overextended. Softly spoken and eager to please, Kundl was as much a caretaker as Günther's latest companion. After the end of his one and only marriage in the early 1970s, my uncle took up with 'a parade of women' (my mother's phrase) happy to clean the house and tend to his needs without asking what was in it for them. When they rumbled him, which they all did sooner or later, they moved on or were replaced by Günther, who was attuned like a spider to changes in his environment, especially if those changes threatened his routine. The quest for a woman who could tolerate him while holding on to a duster had recently foundered with the departure of Olga, a woman who stayed for eight years only to leave after meeting a younger man. Kundl, gentler than previous holders of the office and at home in an apron, was the ideal

41

With the tension aboard the Spanish ships visible in the shape of bitten, bleeding lips and the constant rubbing of sweaty palms on thighs, the Austrians approached. The drums grew louder and louder, joined by the sounds of terrible exertions in the bowels of those ships – like a herd of constipated cows – as the Teutonic oarsmen gave

———————

partner. Not only was she older than my uncle, but she *looked* older, fish-eyed behind thick lenses, tanned skin rippled and loose, her dyed blonde hair lifeless as a wig. She smiled and smiled, nodding as we smiled back.

'Günther hasn't heard us,' my mother said, still nodding at Kundl.

Most of the fifteen rooms were unused. Kundl, their curator, visited different areas on a weekly rota to dust surfaces, polishing metal and shining wood until her piscine face stared back at her. Meanwhile, Günther lay on the bed in his boxy bedroom, the smallest in the house and no bigger than a walk-in wardrobe. Actors screamed at him on television. Now I could hear it, coming from above: gunfire, incidental music, screeching brakes, voices.

'He's turning into an old man,' my mother said, watching Kundl creep upstairs to summon him.

Then he was there, on the landing, Kundl just visible behind him like a courtier.

Still in his pyjamas at two o'clock, the pale-blue polyester jacket open to reveal the dented chest I had inherited, the muscles in his face were hyperactive, trying to convey anything from surprise and outrage to dismay and despair, gesticulating, hands around his head, a cataract of German crashing down on us. The pencil moustache was a little thicker, the black

their all. When, drenched to saturation point from the attentions of dripping palms, it seemed as if Spanish bell-bottoms could take no more, and the throb of drums would deafen everyone, the entire Austrian Fleet arced away, a whoosh of air sweeping over the sweaty faces of the Spaniards, cooling them in an instant. The lit tapers

---

greased-back hair was dyed, the hairline was turning from a minus sign to a V, but he still resembled Clark Gable, albeit the version on his last legs in *The Misfits*. His legs, however, belonged to a man in his thirties, brown, muscular calves shown off by a pair of Bermuda shorts. Amid the downpour of chatter, he descended to the gloomy hall and welcomed us. My father blinked before the imminent flood.

'*Stefanl Wic gehts?*' He crushed my hand with a khaki paw.

'*Sehr gut, danke,*' I replied as he was turning away to begin the tour.

We headed for the kitchen in a crocodile, Günther, my mother, me, my father. When I looked back, Kundl had gone. Long and narrow, the kitchen had a window at one end that looked on to the garden, an ornamental pond, and what could have been a potting shed. A huge sheet of sunlight lay across the lawn, individual blades of grass were visible even from where I stood, at the far end of the room. Inside, it was gloomy.

'He should be growing vegetables,' my mother said, glancing at the dishwasher under her left hand.

'*Sehr schön, jo?*' my uncle said, when he noticed my mother's fingers resting on the reprovingly cold, white metal.

'Günther,' my father chirped, 'new?'

I stood at the door, leaning against the jamb and wondering what to admire when Günther swept past me, back into the

poised above the Spanish cannons were extinguished in an instant and the Admiral's mascot, a parrot called Hernandez, blown from its perch, struck its feathery head on the deck and died.

[I worried about that parrot for days, until my father

---

darkened hallway and up the stairs, muttering as he passed.

The house was cool, dark as an untended aquarium or bright as a goldfish bowl. Lit by a wall-sized window – thick panels of blue, green and yellow glass that warped and diffused the rays of the sun – the landing was dazzling and airless. Wasps died there. He continued his tour in the upstairs lounge, the television and video room where the curtains were permanently drawn. A splinter of sunlight. Hoarded for a life in exile, dozens of home-made video tapes lined the walls. Among the decorative leather-bound books and herds of ornamental elephants shining in the dark, one whole shelf was devoted to nature documentaries. My mother scanned the room for new acquisitions, too irritated simply to ask what her brother had been buying. She knew he would show her sooner or later. China elephants, wooden elephants, elephants made of porcelain, wire and metal, elephants big as cats or small as matchboxes had usurped the satyrs with arched backs and threatening erections on display when I was a child. The bayonet with a swastika on the handle was still there, however, and I wanted to pick it up, to take the blade from the sheath to see if it had rusted.

Images flipped on the television screen as my uncle showed us just how many stations were reaching him, how much news he could hear at the touch of a button. Talking heads, shoot-outs, embracing lovers. From the bowl of stale peanuts

44

assured me it had been a wicked bird that pecked everyone who came near it; everyone, that is, except the Admiral, who was inordinately fond of it. But as the Admiral was not a pleasant man, the loss of the parrot was something I shouldn't mourn too much.]

---

on the glass coffee-table (extra large, sent by my mother) and Günther's unfamiliarity with the satellite channels, it was clear this wasn't a room he often visited. The TV guide on the table next to a mail-order catalogue was three years old.

'Ah, Richard Vidmark!' he yelped, then 'Chessica Fletcher!' when he clicked on a strangely dubbed Angela Lansbury in an episode of *Murder, She Wrote*, her voice too deep, too manly.

Looking for stations we might want to watch – CNN, Sky – my uncle was unwilling to settle on one for long enough to discover its country of origin. When he did locate an English-language programme, he didn't recognize it as such but continued changing channels, his irritation growing, his arm outstretched as though the infra-red beam of the remote control was too feeble to make the entire journey from his creaking, leather swivel-chair to the black panel on the front of the set.

'That's English!' I said to my mother as Günther left one particular news programme for the third time.

My mother reported the fact and he shrugged, said some-thing so quickly that it didn't even sound like words, slapped the remote control on the arm of the chair then stormed out, on to the next leg of our tour.

The floor shook, elephants trembled.

I could hear, from outside, the tap tap tap of the man building a house on the other side of the road, the shuddery clang and thud of metal poles and planks, the thump of something large

'Maintain the stroke,' the Baron cried.

Standing on the prow of his ship like David Niven in his doomed bomber at the beginning of *A Matter of Life and Death*, the wind in his hair, his chin thrust out heroically,

---

reaching the end of a chute then splintering, the chugging of a cement mixer.

On the way to our next port of call we met Kundl on the stairs, awaiting instructions. She was holding a cloth, so it might have been the TV room's day for attention as soon as she received the go-ahead. She smiled as we passed her, in Günther's wake, on to the upstairs bathroom where the floor was wet. One at a time, we poked our heads round the door to admire the lime-green bath and basin, the silvery shower attachment, the pristine shower-curtain decorated with pale flowers. The floor sloped towards a central drainage hole, as though the architect had anticipated very splashy bathers or incontinence. The pipes leading away from the hole began gurgling in time with the faint churnings of the cement mixer opposite, each gulp releasing a wave of rank air no one apart from me seemed to notice. So strong it should have been visible, the smell blossomed and I breathed through my mouth for the next five minutes.

The door to Günther's room was open, the bed unmade, the sheet rippled on the mattress, the bedding curled over like a breaker, the one pillow propped up against the headboard. The three-quarters-closed Venetian blinds only emphasized how poky a room it was. There were loose pages of magazines and newspapers scattered across the floor. The place smelled of sleep and age. At night, the blue flickering of the TV on the blinds and on the ceiling could be seen from the road, the volume so high that dialogue was audible.

The twin beds in my room had been pushed together by

he watched the enemy's vessels pass in a blur. Below decks, his men were too exhausted to feel a sense of shame or betrayal, though they knew they were on a course away from the foe.

Kundl, who presumed I took after the Austrian side of the family. Although the paintwork was fresh, the furniture was 1950s, a featureless wardrobe with matching bedside tables and, puzzlingly, a stool from a long-departed dressing-table, its legs splayed like Bambi's, its buttoned seat covered in a dusty mustard-coloured material. A large blue-china jumbo stood on a shelf above the beds, its rearing trunk attached to its forehead like a handle, and above it hung a specimen of the house's other leitmotif, tapestries of poorly rendered naked women. Framed behind glass, they were displayed on the walls of every room like trophies. My companion for the week, a nude with gravity-defying breasts, reclined on a swag of red velvet, the dog-sized creature at her knees sniffing a letter sealed with wax the colour of her toenails, a pair of swans (a nod to the mythological setting) marooned in the tar-coloured lake over her left shoulder. Behind them all sat something like the Acropolis.

Günther stretched across the bed to demonstrate the concealed light that ran the length of the headboard. He grunted, and a greasy strand of brilliantined hair, dislodged by his flapping hands, dropped before his eyes. It was a wonder he hadn't shaken himself to pieces years ago, like an early flying-machine attempting to leave the ground. My silent father, standing at the door of the bedroom because he hadn't been invited in, looked as lost as Harold Lloyd clinging to the face of a clock.

'Günther's just had this room decorated,' my mother said.

'Maintain the stroke!'

With a single, fluent movement, the drummers with aching arms were replaced, while teams of oarsmen kept in reserve slid into the seats of their exhausted comrades without a stroke being missed.

On they swept, heading north, apparently fleeing the Spaniards who, momentarily stunned by the Austrians'

'Very nice,' I said, breathing through my nose at last.

My uncle fiddled with the light, growled, twitched at his failure, then showed me how the blinds worked and demonstrated how to open the window. It was a simple operation I mastered at the first attempt, although, to satisfy himself, he made me do it again, this time with me talking it through.

'That isn't too difficult, is it?' my mother said.

With both hands, she pulled her lemon cardigan across her giant bosom. Her elbows almost straightened. I could see, across the road, the man working on his house, trundling bricks in a wheelbarrow from one level to another, a little wisp of smoke from a cigarette playing about his face. I remembered looking out of this window when my chest was level with the sill and seeing a field, wild flowers, long grass, then a row of blue mountains we might have visited the day before. Now, there were identical houses everywhere; houses like my uncle's. Whole streets had grown up around Günther. Only a few gaps remained. One by one, they were being plugged.

'This place has changed,' I mumbled.

What the room had been like when I was last in it I couldn't have said, but the dressing-table stool must have been somewhere in there, quietly surviving.

Clearing her throat, my mother rumbled like thunder.

perplexing strategy, gathered their wits and set off in pursuit.

'Spaniards to stern!' an excitable man in the crow's nest of one of the Austrian vessels cried out. 'Ahoy! Ahoy!'

The message was passed from ship to ship until it reached the Baron, looking north and – unbeknownst to anyone, not even his officers – praying for a wind to spare his crew their exertions. Turning, he could see the Spanish Fleet in the distance, specks growing by the minute, and he bowed his head, and locks of hair he had neglected to Brylcreem that morning fell about his face, obscuring his view of the deck. Then, as if in answer to his prayer, a strand of hair lifted. Then another. Then another. Soon his dark mane was off his face and he could see his ship, his men shouting for joy as, yes, there was no mistake, the wind was at their backs, and now the Baron's hair was streaming like a flame.

Wind filled the sails, wind whistled through the rigging, wind caught the Austrian ships and pushed them north, and the drained oarsmen slumped over their oars felt the momentum and stopped rowing, like a boy lifting his feet from the pedals to freewheel on his bike. In every ship of the Austrian Fleet great cheers went up, in every ship the drummers were pelted with sweaty socks and sodden shirts then sent to Coventry.

For three days and three nights the chase north continued. Past Dover, past the north of England and

Scotland, then up the length of Norway the two fleets raced, closer to the Arctic than they had ever been. The sight of snow and giant icebergs made the crews so terribly homesick[7] that they began to sing mournful dirges, awful tunes the Baron had not missed for one second of his mountain-top exile.

On the third night, his ears plugged with wax, he hatched a plan in his candlelit quarters, among the charts of the seven seas and the strata of scented letters from female admirers waiting on quaysides all over the world. Unshaven but resolute, he called his second-in-command.

'Baron.' The second-in-command clicked his heels.

7. Fortunately for us all, my father appreciated the Austrian landscape as much as my mother. He had no choice, of course; anywhere else in the world was rarely an option. He even sat through videos of the Austrian weather forecast Günther sent my parents now and then. *Wetterpanorama*'s cameras, stationed on mountain tops throughout Austria, transmit live images. They pan the countryside remorselessly, like CCTV surveillance. My favourite is the record of a winter morning so cold that ice on the lens or else fog obliterated any view: a series of blank squares pass before the viewer's eyes to a backing track of oompah music.

Including a stopover in a German guest-house, the drive from Wales to Austria took three days. While the autobahns were scary, sutured racetracks, the sun shone on bare stretches of tarmacadam in Austria, the heat-haze warping the air in front of us, the sky an uninterrupted, Hockney blue.

'Isn't it clean!' my father would announce. '*Wunderbar*.'

Roads winding around and up mountains, roads punctuated

'Now we are ready,' the Baron said, both arms on the table, holding flat an unrolled map of the Arctic Circle that curled around his forearms. 'Light braziers in the hold of every ship and place a guard on every one.'

'Baron.'

The second-in-command clicked his heels and left.

The candle flickered in his wake and the Baron closed his eyes, exhaled and rested where he was, upright in his cabin in a high-backed chair. The fires were lit while he slept, so many in every hold that it seemed like daylight in the Sahara, the hull glowing, shafts of light breaking

---

with piles of chopped wood stacked on the verge, roads so mazy it is easy to lose your sense of direction when all mountains begin to look like one mountain, hemmed with woodland and capped with snow. A landscape of absences. No heavy industry, no evidence of tourism, only miles of undulating land with handfuls of buildings in sight at any one time, then miles of pine forests and bluish mountains overlooking photogenic rivers. The buildings, when you reach them, are freshly painted toy-town colours – ochre, pale yellow, pastel blue – the people growing from childhood straight to adulthood. You can study a house but have no idea of its owner's age. Most times, especially around midday, there are no signs of life, a butterfly tottering from one wild verge to another, perhaps, as though an apocalyptic event had removed the people but left the buildings intact. Smoothly denying its own past, idyllic and a little sinister, a country fit for a Stepford wife. 'Land of mountains, land of streams, land of fields, land of spires, land of hammers with a rich future . . .'

through the gaps in the timbers, the air so hot that the guards were there in nothing but their shorts, standing on wet towels stacked ten deep, unable to touch their guns and swords for fear of burning themselves. Even though the bowels of the ship were boiling and the decks were warm to the touch, ice was forming on the rigging and the sea began to thicken the further north they travelled.

Within a day, icicles hung from every sail, the wind dropped, the rigging tinkled and the sailors in the crow's nests were wrapped like Michelin men. The pace slowed. Breath fogged the decks. It was so cold that words froze on sailors' lips before they could be heard. Phrases like '*Guten morgen*' or 'It's cold today' were taken below and thawed out. Gradually, the sea turned to ice, first in the form of shallow rafts but soon as great slabs that clashed like deer.

[My father would bang his fists together at this point and I'd shiver even though a feathery duvet was pinning me down.]

Despite the ice, despite the freezing temperatures, the Austrian Fleet continued north, closer to the pole than any Austrians had ever journeyed before. Soon the ice was all around them, and only the braziers burning below decks, warming the hull of every ship, prevented them from being embraced, held fast in the middle of no-where.

On the seventh day, when progress had slowed to

walking pace and gangs of sailors were sent overboard to push, the Baron spoke to his men:

'*Meine Damen und Herren*,' he said [there were no women on board, but it was a phrase my father knew], 'it is time to finish off the enemy.' He pointed to the Spanish Fleet frozen in the distance, held by the ice that the Austrians had conquered. 'Assemble the boarding parties, Mister,' he said, turning to his second-in-command.

'Baron,' he replied, clicking his heels. Splinters of ice flew off like sparks.

So, boarding parties from all nine vessels were armed to the chattering teeth and sent back to fight the Spaniards on foot. Those left behind stoked the fires or clapped their mittened hands together like a first-night audience at the theatre. They watched their comrades disappear, then waited, speculating on the battle that would ensue on the horizon.

Two days and two nights passed without the distant sounds of gunfire or tell-tale plumes of smoke. Nothing, only the noise of the ice creaking and moaning round the ships, threatening to hug them to pieces if the fires were allowed to die. At the end of the third, brief day, as the sun was setting in purples and golds behind a band of clouds, the Michelin man in the crow's nest shouted out.

'Our boys! Our boys! Ahoy! Ahoy!'

His voice echoed. The crews were roused and the cheering began, cheering that sheared off the faces of icebergs miles away even as the Baron, hawk-like, was counting the men and speculating on the casualties. It was another hour before he could believe his eyes. Not one man had been lost. With a restraint expected of the officers of the Austrian Navy [something my father obviously understood all his life], the Baron greeted his men with a nod of the head and the slightest of smiles, concealing his sense of relief.

'Baron,' his second-in-command said. He clicked his heels but, thick with snow, they made no sound. 'We arrived on the morning of the second day and found no signs of life. Fearing a trap, we proceeded with caution. Circling each vessel, we held our ears against the hulls to listen and it was thus that we sustained our only casualty.' He pointed to one sailor with a bandaged head. 'Fritzy,' he said, 'pressed his ear to the freezing wood and in the icy temperatures it stuck fast. We had no choice.'

There was an intake of breath, sailors taking the freezing clouds back into their lungs as they pictured Fritzy's ear glued to the side of the Spanish ship. From that day forward they would call him Van Gogh [an anachronism I only discovered years later].

'When we heard no sounds, we boarded the first ship. A difficult task, Herr Baron, as the ice was thick on everything. It was then that we discovered the crew, still manning their last positions, at the rigging, in the masts, at the wheel, and in their hammocks, frozen solid and dusted with a fall of snow, several with little pyramids of snowflakes atop their solid heads. Nobody was stirring.

There wasn't a sound. On every ship the picture was the same.'

The lack of winter clothing had put paid to their pursuit. The Baron's strategy had worked.

'Bravo,' the Baron said.

'Thank you, Baron,' the second-in-command replied, too moved to click his heels. 'I brought you this.'

From his bag he took the Spanish Admiral's parrot, stiff as a cricket bat, a look of surprise on its grumpy face. At the sight of this, the entire crew let out a mighty cheer, dislodging fragments of ice from the rigging and masts, showering themselves with white, halving the size of glaciers far in the distance.

They, in turn, were cheered on their return to Austria, news of their triumph preceding them. The burghers of every town and village put out bunting, children acted out the Baron's triumph in playgrounds up and down the country (no one ever wanted to be the Spanish Admiral), and there was yodelling in the streets for days and nights on end. In Knittelfeld, the whole of the Lindenallee[8] was cordoned off for a street party that lasted a week and there was dancing, singing, kite-flying, the works.

By popular demand, a holiday was declared and it was

8. The top-floor flat where my mother's parents lived at the end of their lives was in the Lindenallee: crunchy gravel; a shadowy avenue of trees; blocks of flats in a horseshoe around a patch of unkempt grass; the stone steps up to my

christened Baron's Day. Schools were given a day off and the building of snowmen and the pelting of snowballs was compulsory, but it was in Graz, his home town, that the Baron achieved his biggest welcome. So many medals of all shapes and sizes were conferred on him that, by the

---

grandparents' four rooms echoey in the dark stairwell; the bulging duvet full of feathers and air; attached to the front of their black-and-white television set, the screen that magnified the image, blurring and warping it at the edges to a mono-chrome, psychedelic vortex. The peanut-headed Men from Uncle speaking German!

Revisiting my childhood haunts, I returned there with my parents to see what was left of the place, wondering if anything familiar had survived. I thought I might walk past the buildings without turning my head, like my baffled father on the platform of Swansea station, looking for my mother.

'You can't see the joins,' I said. 'Where the old finishes and the new begins.'

The drab fairy-tale houses had turned from grubby greys and browns to butterfly pastel green and yellow. Like someone checking for traffic, I stood looking up and down the avenue to take my bearings, to recognize the homes I used to circle on my cousin's bicycle, the one I had to lean at an alarming angle before dismounting. Functional, sharp-edged, the super-market opposite the flats was still open and as hatchet-faced as ever. I was taken there as an eight-year-old to be spoilt with sweets or the little polystyrene aeroplanes they sold in two pieces in oblong plastic bags. You slotted the wing into a fuselage weighted at the nose with a metal clip. In the still air of the avenue they floated like a dream. I held on to them for

end of the evening of their presentation, his shoulders were drooping under their weight.

Fireworks lit the night sky, bursting above the onion domes and spires like snowballs breaking against the darkness, while an orchestra played the Baron's Waltz, a

---

years, in a box in the loft where, under the weight of annuals, toys, exercise books and my father's collection of *Amateur Photographers*, they must have disintegrated like the husks of insects.

'They think it's going to close,' my mother said.

The pavements that used to be gravel. The washing-lines that hadn't changed at all, beside the garden allotments that had always been there at the back of the flats. A small hut painted green.

'This was Opa's, wasn't it?' I asked my mother.

My grandfather had been dead for over twenty years but the potting shed he slunk to when my grandmother was in one of her tempers or objected to the stink of his sweat, the place where he used to kill rabbits – holding them up by their soft ears to cut their throats while they kicked their paws in space – was still standing, adrift among the spruced-up homes.

Weedkiller; a crust of earth on the tools; dried blood.

Discovering the tasty stew on my spoon was made from a creature I'd petted the day before, I burst into tears, repeating 'We don't eat our friends . . . We don't eat our friends.'

'He built it fifty-five years ago,' my mother said. 'With the help of the man who lived in that flat.' She pointed to a room on the ground floor just behind us. 'He's dead,' she added.

'It's being so cheerful as keeps me going!' my father chirruped.

57

specially commissioned piece written by one of the umpteen Strausses around at that time (not, it has to be said, one of the more talented members of the family), and the mayor's speech went on for half a day.

Now, every winter, in the heart of Graz, a statue made of ice is raised on a marble plinth bearing the Baron's name above the date and description of his victory. The detail on the statue is always meticulous: the Baron's wild eyebrows and his eagle eyes, the twists and turns of his braided uniform, his mighty sword. In the early years after his triumph, waggish sculptors would add a little parrot at the base, though that disappeared as the details of the story blurred and were lost. In later years, whether his moustache should be bushy as a copse or clipped like a toothbrush was a subject of heated discussion among Austrian patriots in guest-houses all over the land. Nevertheless, what rose up every winter was the Baron in all his glory, watching over Graz through the bitterest months, a giant ice sentinel, a man of the mountains who came down to conquer the foe that was threatening his homeland. *Der weiße Riese.* Every winter he towers above the populace, and every spring he is washed away, limb by limb, down alleyways and lanes, along the kerbs and down the drains, a melancholy reminder that summer isn't far away.

3.

UTE

In the dying days of the nineteenth century, Ute, the youngest daughter of Wilhelm, Admiral of the Austrian Fleet, became a prisoner of her father's twin obsessions, ships and the fear that his favourite girl might one day be spirited away by a wholly inappropriate suitor. Wilhelm dreaded his baby meeting a man who didn't have a steady income, a man who couldn't erect a shelf, a deadbeat, or, worst of all, a German. He settled on a way to combine these two obsessions when the burghers of Maria Wörth[9] offered to pay for the construction of any monument he desired, a gesture of gratitude for one of his great maritime victories against the Swedes. No expense was to be spared.

9. Their plaster smooth as skin, the buildings of Maria Wörth are dazzlingly white and the lake is as clear as air – its pin-sharp reeds, pebbles and trout (placid amnesiacs nudging one another) must have been out of our depth, though it seemed as if we could have knelt on the bridge to dip our hands in the water and touch them. A dozen people hunched up, hands at the ready near hats and plastic headscarves, were squinting into a wind that corrugated the surface of the turquoise lake the afternoon we arrived.

'They call this the Austrian Riviera,' my mother said, reversing into a space in the deserted car park.

'Danke schön,' said Wilhelm.
'Bitte sehr,' said the burghers.

Dirty white pedalos roped to a jetty jostled one another listlessly. A few yachts were being scattered to the shore. My mother dwarfed a burly man peering at the instructions on the ticket machine, prodding what appeared to be – but obviously wasn't – a button, stabbing it with his thumb to no effect. Taking command, she spoke to the man, who shrugged good-humouredly then walked away while the wind finished off the perm she had begun to rub anxiously the day before, her nervous habit from the years of her breakdown. Facing this incomprehensible machine, she began to massage her scalp again, 'to ease the pressure'.

'I can't get this to work. I don't know where my bloody glasses are. Why does he leave everything to me?' she said, rummaging through her handbag. 'Bloody old man . . .'

There were nine years between my parents and hardly a day passed without my mother reminding him of the fact. He had shrunk as he'd aged, while my mother broadened and thickened like a snow drift. She used to delight in reporting the comments of people at work. 'Who was that old man you were with in town?' or 'I saw you with your father yesterday,' though we never knew if she made them up.

At the lakeside café, waiters hastily collapsed sun-umbrellas on the terrace, removing tablecloths the gale was threatening to carry away, or pinning down napkins with salt-and-pepper shakers. A waiter arrived fresh from his struggle, hair sticking up like a punk. (Or 'bunk', as my mother would have said, her accent a curious blend of Austrian and Welsh.)

'These prices are disgraceful . . .' she muttered loudly, hold-ing the menu at arm's length and narrowing her eyes.

After months of consultations with architects, painters, musicians, sportsmen and aficionados of the ballet (Wilhelm was nothing if not thorough), he settled on a huge

---

My father murmured, 'Quiet, Helma, can't you?'

'No wonder they don't get much business,' she said, even louder.

Beyond the lake, black clouds were gathering, circling the range of mountains that themselves encircled the lake. When the waiter returned with our order, my mother struck up a conversation and we fell silent, my father lifting the menu to hide his face then gurning at me rebelliously, poking out the bottom plate of his dentures for his *pièce de résistance*.

Switching to English, 'They aren't coming this way,' she said as the waiter left, then, indignantly, 'I asked for black bread.'

'One thing at a time, Helma,' my father groaned. 'What's not coming this way?'

'Do you want me to call him back?' my mother asked as we bit into our sausages, having wrapped them in chunks of the white bread our waiter had brought. 'Shall I call him back?'

'You're fussing too much, Helma,' my father said. 'That's why he's confused.'

'I asked him for black bread,' she whined.

'What's not coming this way?' I asked.

'The black clouds,' my mother replied, rubbing her head as she turned round in her seat to look for our waiter, who was grappling with an umbrella at the far end of the terrace.

She gave up trying to attract his attention and, disgruntled at first, settled down to eating her sausages, muttering that the bread wasn't fresh or that she'd tasted better meat, until the mass of food in her mouth silenced her altogether.

In the car on the way to Maria Wörth I had recalled one of

metal ship, a landlocked vessel as big as a city, with funnels as tall as the nearest mountain, a hull no shorter than twenty miles [halfway between Swansea and Cardiff, my father helpfully explained], and decks wide enough to stage a Formula One Grand Prix race, if such a thing had existed in 1897.

———————

the photographs in Christl's collection, my parents as a young couple on a beach, which prompted me to ask them again about when and where they had met. Now, without warning, my mother continued reminiscing, her mouth working the food like a cement mixer.

'. . . It was my holiday, and the dentists where I worked said I could go with them to West Wales or I could go home to Austria, but if I went home I had to promise them I'd come back, and I said "I can't do that." Right? "I can't do that." To promise them that I'd come back once I'd gone.'

My mother looked across to my father, who was miles away, his dentures grappling with the crust, his blue eyes starey.

'Why not?'

'I was homesick. I was only staying because of Maria, because she'd met someone.'

Her friend Maria, who had travelled with her from Knittelfeld after the war, went back to Austria within a year, baffling my mother, who was convinced that she would be the one to return home to her parents.

'We met this young airforce man in *Sanct* Helen's Road and he took us to meet his parents, so when it came to our holiday they said, "You can stay here with us."'

By now, my father had finished eating and was listening to the story of his courtship.

64

Enthused by the honour of honouring a hero, the townspeople set to work raising the millions of schillings required. They shattered piggy banks, held raffles in churches, sold flags they attached to lapels with little pins, baked strudels they took to fairs. When the money began to fill the town's coffers, craftsmen travelled from all over

---

'Of course,' my mother continued, 'Maria and I were going out somewhere every day, and that's how I went swimming.'

'How did you get talking to them?' I asked my father.

'Well,' he said, shyly but glad to be included, 'you go in the water and you start talking. When you're swimming about and somebody's in the water, you just start speaking to them.'

'You didn't talk politics in the sea, did you?'

I imagined my parents swapping analyses of dialectical materialism as they trod water, my mother parroting her father, and Dad representing his uncles' opinions.

'No, no,' he said. 'That came later.'

'But you asked her out that day?'

'To the cinema.' He addressed my mother, who was finishing off the bread. 'You couldn't go, could you?'

'I always remember this, what you said about the smell of garlic from me. I mean, I never chewed garlic. But . . . was there a delicatessen where I bought some sausage?'

'No, no, no,' my father muttered, jokingly. 'You've got it all wrong again. She's got it all wrong again, as usual.' Then, out of nowhere, 'I didn't recognize her accent, so I thought she was from North Wales.'

My mother carried on, oblivious to the reprimand, talking about my father as if he wasn't present. 'The funny thing is, if somebody said to me, "What colour are his eyes?" – most

65

the land to contribute to the mightiest engineering feat the world had ever seen. Woodcarvers arrived from the north, intent on sculpting the handrails of every staircase, huge snakes that coiled upwards. Woodcarvers from the south offered intricate designs for the doorknobs, parrots, sloths, the heads of elephants, the tails of peacocks, the face of Wilhelm. Metalworkers shaped then polished brass fittings, nozzles, pipes and rings blossoming un-expectedly from corners like cold bouquets. The enormous plates that formed the hull were hoisted by enormous cranes operated by *Gastarbeiters* (the Austrians were never

---

people notice the eyes, isn't that true? The first time? Was it the cinema? But I noticed how neat he was. What a lovely collar he had on his shirt.'

Around us, used napkins were picked up by the wind and borne away like dandelion seeds, a gust eddying around the tables toppled a chair, a pepper-mill rolled to the edge of a table only to be caught by a waitress at the last moment. The clouds, however, were skirting us just as our waiter had promised they would, blown around the peaks, circling the lake, delivering rain elsewhere.

'It wasn't bad after all,' my father said, as my mother poked at her teeth with a cocktail stick, hiding her mouth with a hand.

By the time we left, a few teenagers were braving the choppy water, diving from a jetty on a private stretch of the lake, then surfacing to throw droplets from their heads like horses. One sat on the edge of the pier, her arms wrapped round herself, her toes just short of the waves. She flinched when her friends made the bigger splashes. They called to her now and then,

ones for the menial task). So gigantic were the funnels that they curved like the surface of the planet itself, so tall were they that ice formed on their rims at the height of summer.

'If anyone stokes the boilers in the engine room,' Wilhelm remarked to his daughter one afternoon, 'the smoke from those giants will blot out the sun.'

'Isn't that how the dinosaurs perished?' his daughter replied, horrified by the monster growing before her eyes.

Her words were drowned by hammering, the creaking of winches and pulleys, the cries of men, sweat shining on their torsos as they raised metal panels the size of

---

lifting their arms from the water to beckon her. No amount of cajoling worked. When one boy ran the length of the jetty to launch himself into space, entering the water in a foetal ball, the huge splash startled the timid girl from the edge.

'Fancy a swim?' my father chuckled, waggling his eyebrows à la Groucho Marx.

Although the guidebooks say Maria Wörth is a *picturesque village set on a rocky promontory, with two pilgrimage churches, all of which have been the subject of a million photographs*, it didn't stop my father placing me shoulder to shoulder with my mother beside the lake to capture their son's return to Austria. His eyes, however, weren't everything they used to be and the snaps he collected from Boots back home were blurred and might have been of anyone.

Back at the café, a waiter vaulted the fence to chase a tablecloth through the car park, sprinting as though his job depended on him retrieving it.

piazzas skyward, shining as though they themselves were metal, iron men building an iron monument for a cold man. Her father eyed those sinewy men with suspicion.

Even before the vessel that would never move was completed, the finest designers in Europe set to work furnishing the hundred State rooms, the thousand bed-rooms with their thousand *en suite* bathrooms – gold taps and gold towel-rails, the bathtubs trimmed with ivory – the fifty ballrooms, the museum, the seven restaurants, the wine cellars, the fourteen guest-houses and the planet-arium. To Wilhelm's precise specifications, the grandest of the rooms was positioned miles from the nearest porthole, at the very heart of the monument, and a thousand animals were to die so that its walls and floor could be covered with their fur. While he sat at his mahogany desk amid an ocean of hooves, skulls and tails, designers paraded past him, each one pulling an animal whose pelt the Admiral would scrutinize.

'*Ja* . . . *Ja* . . . *Ja* . . . *Nein* . . . *Ja* . . . *Nein* . . . *Ja* . . . *Nein* . . . *Nein* . . . *Nein* . . .'

Months passed and, deck by deck, the ship grew out of the once-forested landscape until even the tallest pine trees left standing were dwarfed, matchsticks in the ashtray of the clearing. The mountains at last had a man-made rival for their grandeur. The burghers of Maria Wörth, despairing that the task would ever be completed, thinned their lips and continued with their work, muttering that whatever the Admiral might have achieved for the Empire, it surely wasn't worth all this! The Admiral never doubted that it was.

The Austrians and their *Gastarbeiters* worked in shifts, day and night without a break. When, three years after the first nail was driven into the first batten, the ship towered before them, all but finished, a party was thrown for all those workers who had survived the ordeal. By now, the cemeteries were swollen with men whose hearts had burst, whose muscles had torn, whose lungs had collapsed from working at altitude, high up on the funnels where paint froze on a paintbrush as soon as it was lifted from the pot.

'TO THE DEAD!' the Admiral roared, raising his tankard to the skeletal ranks.

'The dead,' croaked the almost-dead, raising their beakers to the sky, or as close to the sky as their enfeebled wrists and arms could manage.

Each man was fed with a *Brettljausen*,[10] though they were so weak they could barely cut the meat in front of

10. A snack served in Austrian guest-houses. The waitress brings a black loaf in a basket, for the middle of the table, then returns with a knife and a breadboard freighted with cuts of maroon, fatty meat – pork, beef, sausages the colour of dried blood spotted with white ovals of fat – mounds of grated horseradish, logs of gherkins, a single slice of tomato and a nightmarish block of grilled, Styrian cheese melting like the Daliesque utensil left to smoulder in Christl's kitchen. Though, as a child, I might have been coaxed into eating something from the board, I normally pulled a face or clamped my lips

them. Nevertheless, the Admiral was happy. Not only was his monument complete but the remaining workers were too emaciated to pose a threat to his daughter. A single, lovelorn sigh would have drained all their energy.

'Tomorrow, the unveiling,' he boomed. '*Prost!*'

The word 'unveiling' turned the mayor of Maria Wörth, a shadow of the eighteen stones he had been when the project began, a queasy, parroty green. His cheeks prickled in the cold air and then, as he feared the worst, sweat began turning to wafers of ice. 'All this work,' he thought, 'and we have no cloth to cover the ship for the grand unveiling. It would take a piece of material the

---

shut, demanding chips with a haughty expression inherited from my mother.

'You're a spoilt brat!' my father would mutter in his wholly unfrightening way, then turn to my mother to say, 'You've ruined him.' His complaint would elicit no more than a shrug.

The only time I did eat one was with my uncle who, in honour of my return to Austria after decades away, invited the three of us to a guest-house a few miles outside town, where we drove one afternoon halfway through my holiday, pulling up in a bumpy car park booby- trapped with puddles. It had rained more than I ever recalled it raining as a boy, great deluges flooding the roads, the lakes overflowing.

'Nice weather for ducks!' my father trilled.

In the middle of nowhere, the guest-house looked fairy-tale edible, window-boxes spilling red, purple and white phlox, geraniums and petunias, the shy, pre-capitalist tin sign on the wall advertising *Gösser Bier* with spots of rust, the carved

size of Andorra to do the job properly. The material left over could clothe an army.'

'Unveiling?' he whispered, half-hoping the Admiral would hear but not daring to speak too loudly.

'A manner of speaking,' the Admiral chuckled. 'Where would we find a bolt of cloth as wide as the Danube at such short notice?'

'Indeed, indeed,' the mayor groaned, unused to this side of the Admiral after three years of demands, tantrums and violent rows. 'A bottle of champagne will suffice.'

'Indeed,' the Admiral replied, imagining his Ute performing the task. 'A big bottle of champagne.'

---

banisters, the high-backed wooden benches at tables covered with shiny cloths. We found my balding, barrel-shaped uncle inside the door with his lady friend, the somewhat funereal Gerda. Dyed auburn, though in the gloom of the guest-house it was black as a beetle's carapace, her hair was swept back into a pony-tail, the severity of which stretched her face, removing the wrinkles that inched from the corners of her mouth and eyes. She was in her fifties and her top lip was invisible. Despite the ferocity of her hairstyle, gravity was dragging both upper and lower lips down at the corners to impersonate the letter n. My mother, who had never taken to Gerda, referred to her as 'Gerda the Sponger' so often that it was impossible to say one without the other. We had to be careful now that we were all together for the first time. Legendarily strong and ten years younger than my mother, Gerda was the woman my mother might have become if she'd remained in Austria and never had to work. Before the owner showed us to our table,

When, days later, the party had subsided [my father sucked in his cheeks then swayed a little to show the effects of drink on a meagre workforce], dignitaries from all over Austria were invited to the ceremony. They came in carriages, they came in sleighs, the mayor of Vienna arrived in a hot-air balloon that steamed like a horse in the freezing air, and the truly eccentric, priding themselves on their simple, Teutonic ways, slid into town on skis as if they didn't have the money for a more luxurious mode of transport. With his daughter at his side, the Admiral was there to greet them, waving, nodding, raising his

---

they stood by the till, Gerda and my giant mother, greeting one another with respect. Sumo wrestlers before a contest.

'Drinks!' Hari boomed. It was one of his few English words.

I ordered a *Mischung*, my father was persuaded to try *Most* – a cider brewed locally – and my mother called for a giant tankard of beer frothy as shaving-foam. Anticipating our arrival, Hari had ordered a *Brettljausen* each and, along with the expected slabs of meat, they arrived with a bowl of congealed dripping that my uncle, Gerda and my mother soon began applying to the canvas of their bread, great dollops of the stuff. Impasto. Careful, my father stuck with the meat on his breadboard, which he ate daintily, breathing through his nose as heavily as a weightlifter.

'*Stefan!*' my uncle roared. '*Essen!*'

Settling and resettling indecisively, the dancing flies didn't bother Hari, Gerda or my parents, who continued with the meal. Flies were scaling the brown curtains behind them, flies were galloping across the table and heading for the meat, flies

tankard as he stood on the podium before the vessel that blotted out the sun as efficiently as night.

'How much longer must we stay here, Father?' Ute asked, tired of the provincial life in Maria Wörth and yearning for the streets of Vienna, where handsome, barrel-chested hussars flocked to every State occasion like cockatoos.

'Now, now,' her father whispered. 'We must be grateful to the citizens of this *wunderbar* town for raising so splendid a monument in my honour. My honour is, after all, your honour.'

---

were perching on their shoulders, their hair, their laps and their hands. Flies rubbing their wings and legs with glee.

'Pobby Charlton . . . Tennis Law . . .' my uncle exclaimed to my father, who smiled, nodded and widened his eyes all at once. The fact that I had been a fan of Manchester United when I was seven had stuck in Hari's head, so he waved his knife in the air, laughing with a mouthful of dripping, re-enacting, I think, a goal from the 1968 European Cup Final.

Even with my A-level grade-E German, I knew when the talk turned to Lisa, my mother's late sister-in-law, whose grave we had visited earlier that day. We found a bouquet of flowers left by my cousin, Lianne. My uncle became less animated as soon as my mother finished a sentence which incorporated *Blumen* and her niece's name, her tone soft and drawn out, pleading.

Tucking in, 'Is *gut*, yes?' my father half shouted, then smiled again, not knowing what was being said around him.

Hari grimaced; pursed his lips; paused. When he spoke, his voice was neither angry nor sorrowful but a curious mixture of

When the great and the good had taken their seats in the shadow of the biggest ship that has ever existed, a ship so vast that if there had been a second flood the entire population of Austria could have been accommodated on its countless decks (though the honour of steering the behemoth into the sunset would have led, of course, to terrible fights), so heavy that one wondered whether or not it could ever float, Ute swung back the Nebuchadnezzar of champagne on its chain, her two hands cold on the glass, then let it go. It flew from her like a particularly heavy

---

the two, and it was impossible to tell whether his response concerned the death of his wife or the attitude his daughter had adopted since the funeral. Years of private history trickled out in a language I couldn't follow. While I struggled with my meal and the talk, an especially fat fly settled on my uncle's pate then proceeded to clean itself.

I'd already heard a little about Gerda from various members of the family via my mother: that Hari had 'taken up with her' before Lisa had died and that everybody knew; that she had moved in with Hari soon after Lisa's death, upsetting Lianne in particular; that she was a smoker. Gossip was seasoned with details of her ruthlessness, consisting largely of the number of cigarettes she smoked in a day, and the fact that Hari was a pushover. At one gathering where Lisa was present and only just alive, Günther had turned to Gerda and said she was lucky to find a sucker like Hari to spend money on her.

'Which is true,' my mother added, when she relayed the story to my father.

In the 1970s, during my mother's troubles, Hari had stayed

bird, a partridge, perhaps, or an albatross; a bad omen, she thought as she watched it swoop, in slow motion, towards the hull of her father's monstrosity. In the terrible shadow of that monument, her arms were goose-bumped, their downy hairs erect.

When, after what seemed like an eternity, the bottle broke against the prow like a flea biting a whale (plink), many of the dignitaries seated starboard, where the summer sun was shining above the silhouette of the vast construction, didn't even notice. Only as a ripple of

---

on the line more often than the average Austrian male could have been expected to (the telephone bills were enormous), listening to my mother groan, my mother wail, my mother incoherently drunk on the other end. She had reason to eye with some suspicion this woman who remained impassive at the mention of graves, flowers, and a dead wife. On closer inspection she looked like a cadaverous version of Lisa, the same hair, the same build, her quietness in company, though, unlike Lisa, she was fond of gold jewellery. Pieces on her ears and neck, a knuckleduster's worth of rings, lumpy garish things topped with semi-precious stones. Busy with the *Brettljausen*, she said little, but when she did speak she revealed the most unfortunate feature of her whole face, an eye complaint that prevented her from looking straight ahead. To talk to you she would have to turn away, as though offering her cheek, then consider you askance. Perhaps the flies on her plate weren't troubling her simply because she couldn't see them.

'Stefan! Essen!'

Hari was pushing the bowl of lard in my direction, his gesture

applause lapped towards them did they join in with the celebration, as grateful to warm their hands by clapping as they were to show their appreciation of the citizens of Maria Wörth and the deeds of the Admiral, deeds which, by this stage, had to be recounted in laborious detail to the younger generation, who were only dimly aware of this elderly hero's achievements. While pockets of the audience in their finery and gloves showered the occasion

---

interrupting the toilet of another fat fly squatting on the beer mats stacked in the middle of our table.

'*Nein danke*,' I said. '*Ich bin* . . .' I patted my stomach and puffed out my cheeks with a gentle 'whew'.

He laughed, continuing to offer lard with one hand while pointing to the last chunk of black bread in the basket.

'*Aber* . . .'

I was saying *wirklich* rather feebly, which Hari probably interpreted as politeness, so he shrugged and continued eating, mopping up what was left with that piece of bread, and the conversation turned to the cost of a *Brettljausen* in the local guest-houses, how poor the meat was in one place, how overpriced for tourists it was somewhere else. There was no end to their outrage, their feeling that the world had turned upside-down.

So animated was the discussion, so indignant were the raised voices, that my father could have been forgiven for assuming he was being excluded from a debate about the resurgence of the Right in Austria or the situation in former Yugoslavia, things he would have liked to talk about if only the vocabulary was at his command and if only the company had been interested. We were sitting a couple of hundred miles

with applause, bubbles of champagne trickled down the hull.

[Like flies walking down the Empire State building, my father added, keen to remind me of the scale of the ship.]

Next came a tour of the vessel, a journey that took three weeks of constant travelling to complete. The servants of the dignitaries packed food (none of the two dozen

---

from a war zone, near the southern border, sealed from time to time to prevent an influx of fleeing civilians, yet the subject of Bosnia only arose in the context of asylum-seekers. Translating on behalf of my father and me, my mother reiterated that you shouldn't leave your umbrella lying on a wall in the vicinity of a refugee, her brother adding that a friend of his watched a gang of them taking discarded kitchen furniture from a skip outside his flat. Television regularly showed the evidence of neighbour killing neighbour, bullet scarred walls, craters in the middle of empty roads and corpses strewn around Sarajevo, amongst bus stops and department stores like looted mannequins, but the talk was mostly gossip – the cost of living, and the wealth of the local dentist, about whose income they speculated, guesswork informed by the knowledge that he'd recently bought a yacht.

'Sehr schön, jo,' Gerda muttered, which must have confirmed her avariciousness in my mother's eyes.

That Austria is landlocked was apparently no obstacle to this display of conspicuous consumption. There are always the lakes to sail from shore to shore, never going anywhere but enjoying the breeze on deck, the admiring glances of tourists in pedalos, the thought of his bank balance fresh like

kitchens was finished), and horses were provided for the long trek between chambers. The clanging of hooves thundered down steely corridors, reverberating through the decks like the shivering of an ogre with flu, and, as if in a sacred place, everyone whispered, afraid to set the echoes murmuring.

'Why must I come . . . come . . . come . . . come?' Ute enquired of her father on the second day out.

the spray in his face, his gold tooth winking like a lighthouse.

I looked again at Gerda, confident that, although she had faced me for most of the meal, I had been as good as invisible to her. She had finished eating without saying much. Her teeth were very white and straight, I could see them clearly as she applied a cocktail stick to their nooks and crannies then, satisfied the last bits of flesh had been extracted, lit a cigarette. Her smoking was one of the first things my parents had told me about her. My asthmatic father mocked her addiction.

'*Gerda* Lindley, she smokes like a chimney . . .' he sang one time, his version of a sixties novelty record by The Singing Postman.

My mother's dislike, on the other hand, was familial and irrational, the feeling that Gerda had moved in on Hari before Lisa's side of the bed was cold. She moaned about the stink around her brother's bungalow, moaned that Gerda couldn't go twenty minutes without lighting up, moaned that Gerda did nothing in the garden. Or just moaned. Now here Gerda was, puffing a long cigarette with narrow bands of red and green, like a simplified rainbow, where the filter ended; a brand which Gerda made regular trips across the border to former Yugoslavia to buy. Watching her smoke, it wasn't difficult to see

'You must . . . must . . . must . . . must,' the Admiral replied, and an elderly civil servant looked around, convinced that someone was suspended, bat-like, from the ceiling, whispering to him.

As various as the rooms were — a safari chamber with raffia matting, potted ferns, rattan chairs and mosquitoes; a Winter Wonderland suite with chairs, tables and twin beds sculpted from blocks of ice; a library the size of the

---

why she was prepared to travel miles for a drag. Her whole upper body lifted when she inhaled, her shoulders rising, her chest collapsing until, after an eternity of hoarding smoke among the soft caves of her internal organs, she narrowed her narrow eyes then tipped back her head, sending a fountain to the ceiling. Then it was a beatified Gerda bringing her head forward, the merest wisp of smoke curling from her nostrils, the tail of a mouse. My mother's mouth crinkled.

Becoming noticeably more animated, tipsy on two glasses of *Most*, forgetting his brother-in-law's limited English, my father buttonholed Hari.

'In four years' time. I will be getting a GOLD MEDAL. For being married to a Mödritscher. For FIFTY years.'

Hari smiled uncomprehendingly.

'FIFTY YEARS,' he repeated, even louder.

'He can't understand you,' I murmured.

'*Eine*. . . GOLD. . . MEDAL,' my father repeated.

Lifting her head from her breadboard — she was polishing off the meat I couldn't finish — my mother let go a deep rumble of laughter, rolled her eyes in comic irritation, then translated on his behalf. Hari chortled at my father's claim while Gerda lurked in a shroud of smoke. I was looking through

79

Albert Hall with row on row of bare shelves awaiting leather-bound volumes; chambers papered with sheet music in tribute to Beethoven and Mozart; replicas of the bedrooms of the kings of Spain, France, Russia, England, Belgium and Peru – the guests became restless by the middle of the second week. Longing for their own beds with their own pillows and sheets [my father must have put this detail in because he knew I was homesick], not to mention the ministrations of their personal chefs and

---

the haze for signs of her relationship with Hari, her hand on his hand, a shared smile, a brief meeting of their eyes (unlikely), but there was little evidence of what they saw in one another. Hari's generosity, his easy-going manner, were obvious attractions, but what she offered him continued to escape me.

After half an hour, the food had gone.

'That was . . . EXCELLENT,' my father announced, groping for a German word lodged at the back of his mind. '*Wunderbar*,' he added softly, when only I was listening.

Despite her protestations that she wasn't hungry, my mother had devoured two meals, my breadboard alone showing signs of pernicketyness: worms of rind cut from the meat, pieces of crust, a gherkin. The owner, a broad lady in a dirndl who might have been eating her profits, came across to ask if we'd enjoyed our food. Hari insisted on paying. We thanked him with a profusion of head-nodding and smiles and, in his turn, Hari apologized for having to leave. With somewhere to go, he and Gerda rose from the table in a cloud of napkins, crumbs and flies as our chairs scraped the tiled floor. Diplomacy was never conducted with more courtesy. The Baron in exile could not have expected more from his Emperor.

food-tasters, they muttered dissent in the tail of the convoy.

'We've been this way before . . . fore . . . fore . . . fore,' the deputy mayor of Freistadt grumbled, his voice like a stuttering golfer's, his ornate beard losing its contours for want of the shaving skills of his personal barber.

'I know . . . no . . . no . . . no . . . no,' his counterpart from Riegersburg groaned.

'The best is still ahead of us . . . us . . . us . . . us,' the Admiral declared, aware that the ranks, disgruntled at being herded together, were restless. 'This way . . . way . . . way . . . way.'

Fortuitously, ahead of them lay the room at the heart of the ship, the room the designers had lined with fur, the room that was miles from anywhere, the warm room, the room where light — reflected down tubes and tunnels from the portholes located miles away — met in a dazzle, bright chopsticks of light, light glittering on the metal rails and pillars that climbed from the ocean of fur swirling around the room in currents capable of dragging a dignitary under.

'A marvel!' exclaimed the Dutch ambassador, a man not given to exclamations.

The dignitaries stood around, their boots in their hands, knee-deep in fur, agog at the opulence. Only the sneezing of an allergic minority prevented the atmosphere from being entirely magical.

'My dear,' the Admiral announced, turning to his

daughter as if she were an audience of thousands, sweeping his right arm around the room like a ringmaster, 'your chamber.'

Wading through the fur of a thousand dead animals, stroking the chilly, golden pillars that supported the ceiling and the canopy of the hairy four-poster bed, none of the assembled crachach observed the look of horror that passed across Ute's face like the shadow of an immense ship.

'Oh,' she murmured.

The sound was swallowed utterly by the hirsute walls.

'You shall be my monument's caretaker,' her father continued, oblivious of the tear forming at the corner of his daughter's left eye like a seed pearl. 'There could be none abler.'

'A wonderful choice,' the mayor of Enns, the oldest city in Austria, chimed, lasciviously stroking his walrus moustache as if imagining the nubile Ute supine in her downy surroundings. '*Wunderbar.*'

[This must be one of my additions. I can't believe my father would have included such racy detail.]

So, unpacking Ute's dresses, shoes, samplers, zither, watercolours and romantic novels from the pack-mule that had been lugging them around uncomplainingly for days on end, the servants bade a sad farewell to their mistress, shaking their heads in disbelief, tutting under their breath. Ute had wondered why her father insisted she travel with all her worldly possessions. Now she knew.

The thought of the decades stretching ahead of her like the chain of the world's longest anchor tipped Ute over the edge and into the arms of her father.

Softly, so as not to embarrass the Admiral, 'Please,' she moaned, 'no. I can't stay here. I can't.'

Her father, mistaking her grief for a reluctance to be parted from her beloved father, gently untangled her arms from his beribboned body, saying, 'Hush. Hush now. I'll visit you. You'll never want for anything.'

It was impossible to tell from his cooing voice or the compassionate uptilt of his eyebrows whether or not he was being honest. Did he really believe this was for the best, or was he simply locking her away from the rest of the world for his own reasons? No one present, not even his daughter, would have been able to say. Most didn't even notice the exchange, while a couple of little dukes, up to their necks in fur, were oblivious of everything except their tickly noses. Their hands at their sides, they extended their bottom lips and blew short puffs of air to dislodge the down.

Ute crumpled to the welcoming floor, unable to say another word or even watch the party leave the chamber in single file, struggling to put their shoes back on without slowing the procession. Her father, at the back of the line that was leaving that room for ever, turned back to look at her; but her face, unfeeling, was buried in fur. As man and beast reached the corridor outside, boot and hoof clanged on the iron floor once again. Their departure could be heard by Ute for a full hour, echoey in the distance like the sea.

The shafts of light in the chamber dimmed. When Ute looked up again (she didn't know how long she had slept) the chamber was illuminated by rows of fat candles fixed to the walls. She hadn't noticed them before, nor noticed the way the fur had been cut to a short back and sides below the candles, where the wax was falling. Already, little mountains of cold wax were growing at the foot of each flambeau, layer on layer piling up, cooling as she watched the drip, drip, drip accumulate, turning dull and hard as her eyes. They reminded her of the world outside, of the hills she used to walk among as a child, of home, and she bowed her head again in disbelief, her heart hardening against her beloved father second by second as the ticking wax climbed towards the ceiling . . .

[In one version of the story, Ute hears a distant tapping noise after a year aboard the ship, a year in which the only visitors are her father (twice) and the cooks bringing fresh provisions; but the meals are always cold by the time they arrive and, worse, the loaves of bread are furry with mould.

Leaving her chamber, she investigates. Her journey lasts five days and nights by torchlight, down into the bowels of the ship. Spiders have been busy and her path is blocked by veils of cobwebs, a wedding dress she pushes past. Dead flies hang from her matted hair. She follows the sound of metal on metal and, now and then, fragments of a song: 'Please release me, let me go . . .'[11] the voice croons from the void.

11. Accumulated over the years, my mother had a wide selection of soundtracks for her sorrowful existence. 'Release Me', Englebert Humperdinck's 1967 hit, was an obvious choice for the early years, played in conjunction with what my brother called oompah music, four albums of identical songs from the mountains: tubas, accordians, guitars and helium-voiced vocalists who whooped, doodled (melancholy, free-form yodelling) or slapped their thighs in time. Steirisch Gmüatlich, by Die Seckauer Musikanten, included 'Mein Schönes Steirerland' and 'Gruß der Heimat', while the highlights of Die Original Lustigen Obersteirer's Mein Schönes Alpenland numbered 'Gruß aus Graz' and 'Mach dir keine Sorgen'. They were tunes dripping with homesickness performed by people who had probably never been further than Greece on their holidays. No words can convey how piteous this music sounded, drifting through the house on a Sunday afternoon when my mother, drunk after lunch, moped around in her apron with the map of Austria on the front.

A more surprising favourite was my copy of Queen's 'Bohemian Rhapsody', played largely for Freddie Mercury's sobbing 'Mama, ooooooo' midway through the song. She played it over and over in the mid 1970s, lifting the needle up then replacing it on the vinyl three or four times in one session, sometimes before the song had finished. She wasn't too fond of Brian May's slashing guitar solo at the end, but, like Freddie, she sometimes wished she'd never been born at all.

This was some time after her father then her mother died

In the bilges she discovers, waist-deep in a muddy concoction, a handsome workman who hasn't realized that the monument is finished. He is attempting to drain the ship of water – seeping up, mysteriously, from the land below – with only the help of a rusty bucket. It's clinking on the floor as he scoops a murky bucketful up before pouring it out of a hole in the hull through which daylight is pouring. She stands for a moment, halfway down the flight of stairs that leads to her future companion, unable to speak. Then, slowly, he turns to her, smiling as if he knew she had been there all along.

How the man had survived without food, my father never explained, which I felt was a flaw.

– Years later, I saw the German director Peter Stein's production of Eugene O'Neill's *The Hairy Ape* at the National Theatre, and was struck by how much one scene, among the stokers, reminded me of Ute and her workman, though I couldn't believe my father knew the play and was plagiarizing the American dramatist. It was something that would never have interested him.

---

within a year of one another, events from which my mother never recovered. She would drink gin, vodka, whisky and sherry to forget, play music to remember, then topple on to the bed like George Orwell's felled elephant to howl and howl for hours at a time, sometimes through the night. Aged twelve, I didn't know what to do, so I stuffed my ears with cotton wool then sandwiched my head between two pillows.

So Ute fell hopelessly in love with the man. They married and had seven children, only leaving the monument over a decade later, with a long-haired brood in tow looking for their grandfather. Even though they might have been intent on who knows what sort of savage reunion, I didn't like this ending and told my father it was soppy.

I was a heartless child.]

4.

FRED

In the late eighteenth century, when the Austrian Navy ruled the seas from the Alps to the Ukraine, lording it over countries twice as big as their own, the one real threat to their authority was the infamous buccaneer Fred the Unspeakable. A pirate who marauded the coast of Austria for seven years, wreaking havoc among merchant ships that cursed the Navy for their lack of protection, Fred mysteriously disappeared after a furious battle at sea, never to be seen or heard of again.

Many rumours grew up around this pirate, rumours that encrusted the facts like barnacles on a keel until Fred was a legend, a sea-going master criminal who was strangely amiable with the crews of captured vessels and rarely made anyone, not even the vilest ship's captain, walk the plank. What no one except a few of the most senior figures in the Austrian Admiralty knew, however, was that Fred was really Elfrieda, a woman from the banks of the Klopeinersee who, considering herself wronged by the Empire, embarked on a revenge that was to make her the scourge of the Seven Seas. My father had seen documents considered too sensitive to acknowledge even in the Austria of 1967, 170 years after the events took place. Though

Fred is hardly acknowledged by the history books, every year, on the same day in November, a sailor's grave[12] is strewn with flowers and moss is picked from what remains of the inscription.

Born Elfrieda Hansi Vogel, Fred had been married to Heinz Vogel, a young naval rating who joined up to see the world, confident that his talents would promote him through the ranks until he was master of his own ship. This, alas, was never to be.

Heinz's first posting was aboard the *Tirpitz*, a cruiser commanded by a notoriously unpleasant captain called

12. Death is almost as popular as skiing in Austria and, of all Austrians, the Viennese are the downhill champions of mortality, visiting the dead at every opportunity but especially on All Saints' Day, when cemeteries are packed with mourners lighting candles. Connoisseurs, they relish the Kapuziner crypt where the sarcophagi of the old imperial family are lodged. When the Habsburg emperors died, they were chopped up and their bits and bobs distributed around the capital, spreading themselves thin for their subjects: their hearts in silver urns to the Church of the Augustinians, their entrails to the catacombs of St Stephen's, and the leftovers for the royal crypt. When commoners take a plot in any of the capital's forty-six cemeteries, on the other hand, they acquire a ten-year lease and, after a decade, have to pay again or forfeit the grave, after which the headstone is removed and the plot sold to someone else.

Vienna's relationship with the dead goes back to the eighteenth century and Emperor Josef II, who hit on the idea

Rolf, a glass-eyed sadist who so resented his binocular crew that he manufactured reasons to punish them at every possible turn. If their hair was greasy, he scolded them with his cruel tongue. If they walked in a way he didn't like, he demoted them. If he suspected them of farting in his presence – even if there was no audible evidence, nothing beyond a peculiar look on a sailor's face and the merest whiff of something on the breeze – he punished them. Nothing was too trivial to bring down his wrath on the hapless crew, who rued the day they signed on to serve with him.

---

of saving money with the recyclable coffin. Placed in a sack, the deceased was inserted into a coffin with a hinged underside that was suspended over a trench until the cadaver dropped through. The box was taken away for re-use. The innovation lasted no more than a year, when the imperial edict had to be revoked because of popular revulsion.

Knittelfelders seem no less conscientious than the Viennese, I realized when I visited my Aunt Lisa's grave. The sky was charcoal, rags of low cloud obscuring the mountains, but the rain was holding off when we arrived at the cemetery on my fifth morning there, parking beside a meadow of flowers (on sale to the visiting bereaved) opposite the main gate. My father groaned as he climbed out of the car.

'I don't know why,' he muttered under his breath so my mother would hear only a growl of discontent, 'we have to come here every year.'

Even in the cinereous light there was the whiteness I recalled from childhood. White gravel paths, white marble

'*Warum?... Warum?... Warum?...*' they muttered at night in their sleep, like a grid of sports cars at the beginning of a race.

The punishments confronting them every day were many and terrible. Sitting in the crow's nest for hours at a time without a vest was only the mildest. The worst included cleaning the deck with your tongue, a chore few survived without permanent scarring and a horrible taste in their mouths.

---

headstones, ranks of black and grey crosses, or springboards pointing at the sky.

Remembering I was there for the first time in years, 'It's very clean, isn't it?' he added cheerily.

Grids of immaculate streets and avenues, Austrian cemeteries are constructed like Manhattan. There are photographs on the headstones, ghostly faces from the early years of the century and, somehow less spectral, the 1970s lapels and bad haircuts of the Bee Gees era. Their photographs showing them in uniform (one a member of the Wehrmacht, the other three SS), the empty graves of four brothers killed on the Russian Front are tucked away in one corner with the other soldiers. It isn't the kind of company my grandfather would have wanted to keep for all eternity, bones or no bones, but he and my grandmother are there none the less. Buried when I was ten, they died within eight months of one another.

More recently, my Aunt Lisa had arrived – so recently that, despite directions from Christl, my mother was having difficulty locating her – though we began by heading straight for my grandparents' stone. My mother could have found it with her eyes closed. While I collected one of the bright-red watering-

One day in the second year of his tour of duty, Heinz was writing home to Elfrieda, the childhood sweetheart he had married during his last shore-leave six months earlier. It was the sort of soppy letter my father threatened to relate in detail if I didn't close my eyes. Thankfully, he never did. Needless to say, it must have been an epistle full of lovey-dovey language, raindrops, roses and whiskers on kittens, composed in his hammock below deck one stormy afternoon off the coast of Lichtenstein. The waves

---

cans provided by the cemetery, she tended the grave, clearing away the previous month's brittle flowers, removing dead leaves and twigs, emptying the dregs from the vase. By the time I returned, she had begun arranging the thin branches of pine tree picked that morning, stopping for me to fill the vase with water.

Scrunching a leaf in her fist, she murmured, 'Hari should visit more often.'

My father stood two plots down from us, studying an inscription as though it were a timetable.

'Let's not hang about, Thora,' he said. 'It's going to rain.'

My mother was placing the twigs one by one, with a care that took no account of the storm that would ruin her arrangement as soon as we'd left. Unable to join in, embarrassed by it all, my father strolled off down an avenue of stones, using his umbrella as a walking-stick, lifting it off the ground with every stride in a jaunty, devil-may-care manner. It was difficult to tell, because of the breeze, but he might have been whistling.

I looked over the crop of headstones. The place was not only more crowded but somehow drabber, nothing like as impressive as my memory of it. Perhaps I saw it last in sunshine,

rocked him vigorously, a rocking that never sickened him, though his quill pen sailed across the parchment, complicating his endearments. The curls and tails of individual letters swooped over the paper like Spirograph patterns, doubling up on one another until few words were visible, though *Love* was always legible.

Trying to forget his nauseousness, '*Was machts du?*' the green-faced man throwing up in the hammock asked

―――――――

when the stones glowed and the photos on the tombs seemed like heavenly passport-snaps; when, of course, I was shorter, and would have been face to face with the dead, not looking over their heads while swinging an empty, red watering-can.

My mother stood. Despite a wind frisking the leaves of trees leaning over the flaking cemetery wall, I could hear her knees click as she rose. We went in search of Lisa's final resting place, my mother leading the way, my father dawdling.

'It's six up and two across, isn't it?' she said, repeating Christl's directions to Lisa's plot. 'Six up and two across,' as though it were an incantation that could make the grave appear, or else the key to a pirate's treasure-map.

'Is it?' my father said. 'I don't remember.'

It wasn't long before anger clouded my mother's face, narrowing her lips, quickening her breathing, tensing her jaw until the sinews in her neck were visible like the strings of a musical instrument. She was angry with us for not being able to find a grave that only she had ever seen, angry at the grave for having slipped its moorings, angry at the sky, angry with my father for being no help when she needed him, angry with the dead. Taking our bearings from a tree at the heart of the cemetery, we repeated Christl's mantra, counting off the

Heinz, when Captain Rolf entered to inspect their quarters for crumbs.

Unfortunately for the two sailors, the captain was strutting past them just as Heinz's slack-jawed shipmate threw up, showering with vomit not only the captain's shoes but also the posh leggings his wife had given him for his last birthday. Rolf stopped in his tracks and, in what seemed like an eternity for the bilious sailor and

---

avenues of headstones as we walked, the gravel underfoot still squelchy with the previous night's rain.

'It must be wrong,' I said. 'Why don't we go now and double-check with Hari this afternoon?'

'I can't do that. I told him I'd put flowers on her grave.'

My mother would not be shifted from her quest. She had an appointment with Lisa's remains and meant to keep it no matter how long it took.

'Six up. Two across,' my father called.

By now, he was lagging so far behind that we'd pass him going in the opposite direction, oblivious to us. I watched him walk sideways down a row of graves, leaning forward to make absolutely sure this wasn't the one we were looking for, lifting his spectacles to his forehead, straightening up, then taking several paces to the side as though about to do-se-do the tombstones. Ignoring my mother's stentorian chant to range to the farthest corners of the cemetery, I spent longer than was necessary studying a tall, black tomb on which ivy encroached. Millimetre by millimetre, tendrils were travelling across the inscription in a painstaking act of censorship, blotting out the family name. The plot looked in danger of repossession.

Passing me, 'Schultzy's *non compos mentis*,' my father

Heinz, slowly sent his chin to his chest to point his one, good eye towards the mess at his feet.

'*WAS* . . .' he thundered, louder than the waves bashing the side of the hull, '*IST . . . DAS?*'

'Puke, sir,' said Heinz, who should have known better but couldn't resist stating the obvious.

No words came from the lips of Captain Rolf at that moment.

[Instead my father demonstrated the depths of his anger by inhaling until his chest was as big and round as a barrel – in those days, his lungs were still good – then widening his eyes till the whites were visible all the way round the blue irises. He held that look of fury for a

---

muttered, then leant towards another headstone. 'Touched. Oh yes yes yes.'

As the first spots of rain began to fall I saw my mother a way off, talking to an old lady, her umbrella up in anticipation. She pointed to an area we hadn't searched. Nodding, my mother marched off.

'Your mother got it totally wrong. She doesn't listen, that's her trouble.'

At her side, wheezing slightly (the kittens in his chest scratching to escape), my father watched her bend to pluck a weed then place flowers in the one vase that was empty, the vase moss was beginning to upholster. Although she'd only been in Knittelfeld overnight, my cousin Lianne had managed to visit her mother, leaving a bunch of lemon gladioli.

'She's a neighbour of Kundl's,' my mother said, referring to the woman who'd pointed the way and was even then stooping

98

whole minute and I knew that Heinz, not the sailor dabbing bits of carrot from his lip, was in trouble.]

'*MEIN . . . GOTT!*' Rolf eventually roared, releasing the pressure from his face. His pink, chubby cheeks trembled like a kettle on a gas ring. 'WOLFGANG!'

A loathsome creature the crew hated at least as much as if not more than their captain, Wolfgang was the captain's scrofulous sidekick. He scuttled like a spider.

'WOLFGANG!' Rolf shouted again, and the obsequious creature that stopped at the captain's right shoulder – coming no higher than his chest – was more repellent than Heinz had remembered.

Seeing the mess on his captain's boots, Wolfgang tilted

---

to groom a relative, disappearing from sight like a magician.

Everyone knew everyone else in town, including the addresses of the dead. Lisa was buried with her father and, unlike my grandparents, had her picture on the headstone, an oval portrait held in a bubble of clear enamel that reminded me of the paperweight kit I played with as a child. It would last for years.

Lisa was just as I had remembered her, dark hair, kind eyes, though slightly rounder in the face; a symptom of the illness that was to kill her at fifty-three. Beside her, her father looked no older. *Alles in Ordnung*. There was no work needed, Lianne had seen to everything the day before.

'Will you visit my grave when I'm dead?' my mother asked in her woebegone voice, the wind shaking a few more leaves from the trees as I rolled my eyes in lieu of a reply. 'Even if I'm buried here?'

forward slightly, as if about to kneel then clean the leather with his tongue, a task the little creep would undoubtedly have relished.

'Wolfgang,' the captain continued, passing up the opportunity to humiliate his horribly faithful officer. 'This sailor is to be punished in the severest manner possible. See to it.'

Heinz gawped at the fat index finger of Rolf pointing straight at him, unable to believe his eyes and ears.

'*Aber . . .*' he stuttered, '*aber . . .*'

Before he could say another word, four burly sailors emerged from the shadows behind Wolfgang and strode towards Heinz. Everyone's faces — Wolfgang's, the thuggish sailors', and Rolf's, with its one, sparkly bulb — shone in the greasy light of the candle that flickered but continued burning throughout the captain's performance.

'*Bitte, Kapitan,*' Heinz pleaded, '*Ich habe eine junge* bride.'

'Take him,' Wolfgang squeaked, twitching his rat-like nose, enjoying his power.

So Heinz was hauled away by the bulgy-muscled men to a fate that none of the crew would ever speak of, even in old age, when they probably could have done so without the risk of the evil but long-gone Rolf forcing them to lick the fo'c'sle.

[I pleaded with my father to reveal the fate of Heinz, but he never would, deeming it unsuitable for my young but surprisingly large ears.]

A year later, Elfrieda received a water-damaged envelope

postmarked from an island in the Spanish Main, on the back of which was written *I'm so sorry I was sick*. Apart from Heinz's last, squiggly letter (the only readable words of which were *Love* and *Sauerkraut*, no matter how much Elfrieda stared at it with or without a magnifying glass), there was also official notification from the Austrian Navy that Heinz was never returning home, a cold document that seemed to mock the scribble over which Elfrieda wept.

Elfrieda was boneless with grief.

[It is a strange fact, but my father's impersonations of grief were very much like the faces he pulled for speechless anger. When he insisted he could have 'trodden the boards', I very much doubted him.]

Nothing but the last letter was ever returned to Elfrieda. Nevertheless, she paid for a tombstone out of the money they had saved for their honeymoon and every morning, dressed from head to toe in black, visited the grave. The fresh flowers she laid were picked on the way to the cemetery in the middle of the little town where they were going to live when Heinz had retired from his position as, they had fantasized, an Admiral in the Austrian Navy.

'*Guten morgen, Liebling*,' she would always begin, then talk to the stone for a good hour; gossip mostly, although, more often than she would have liked, a stream of invective bubbled over the grave like clean, Austrian mountain water.

Time set to work smoothing the corners of the headstone. As much as she tried to stop it, snow and rain ate the letters of her husband's name, determined to erase it from the face of the earth. Months passed, but the anger in Elfrieda's heart did not. Even before the first anniversary of the disappearance had arrived, the name on the gravestone read

HEINZ ARTHUR VOGE

RIP

One afternoon, home from her husband's empty plot where a thunderstorm had raged around her, Elfrieda towelled her hair dry in the bedroom of her small cottage on a mountain above the town. Muttering to herself, as she always did, Elfrieda cursed the Austrian Navy and the glass-eyed monster who had taken her beloved. This afternoon, perhaps because of the sopping clothes that clung to her so unpleasantly, she stamped her feet on the wooden floors as she dried herself. A symptom of neglect, dust billowed up. With a creak barely audible above the thunder, the wardrobe door swung open just as a bolt of lightning lit the gloomy room. The uniform her late husband had bought optimistically in preparation for his life as an Admiral glowed on its hanger, the buttons blazing in the eerie light.

'*Gott in Himmel*,' she murmured, as a rumble of thunder rolled over the house like a very noisy neighbour shifting furniture upstairs.

There and then, Elfrieda conceived her revenge on the whole world for depriving her of happiness. With an odd solemnity, she lifted the uniform out of the wardrobe, caressing it tenderly. A clap of thunder shook the house. Slowly closing the wardrobe door, she stood before its full-length mirror, holding the uniform up in front of her. By the time the next bolt of lightning was spookily illuminating the room, she was slipping it off its hanger, telling herself that, with a few alterations, the unworn uniform would fit her perfectly. She was a big lady, so the length of the arms and legs would be no problem.

She set to work that very afternoon, cutting and stitching, adding extra braid she found in her kitchen, dyeing the cuffs of the shirt blood-red, sewing a skull and crossbones on the tricorn hat, squinting in the fading light, stopping only to circle herself with candles. She worked for hours without food and water, transforming the uniform into a parody of its former self. It was the first stage of her revenge.

As she towered in front of the mirror, '*Nichts mehr Elfrieda*,' she boomed, deliberately deepening her voice. '*Ich bin* . . . FRED!'[13]

Outside, birds were singing, the sun was glimmering on the mountain ridge at the back of the house, and

13. I was, from an early age, fascinated by secret identities. All my favourite heroes from the glossy-covered American comics had one. They were either costume disguises like Bruce Wayne's Batman outfit and Clark Kent removing his spectacles

the music of distant cow-bells drifted over the springy meadows like a shower of ice, as it did the following morning when a farmer herding cattle to upland pastures watched a broad-shouldered man in uniform, a man he had never before seen, lock the door of Elfrieda's shuttered house then walk down the gravel path with a large bundle, never once looking back.

In the months that followed, Fred haunted the docks of a dozen Austrian ports looking for passage to Belgium, intent on leading a crew to mutiny under 'his' command and becoming the terror of the Austro-Hungarian Main.

---

before donning his Superman cape, or else there were physical transformations: Dr Blake banging his gnarled walking-stick on the ground to become the Mighty Thor, or, when angered, Bruce Banner, the hapless victim of his own experiment with gamma rays, whose pectorals and biceps expanded until they burst his shirt, leaving it in tatters, his green skin revealing him to be the Incredible Hulk.

Half-Austrian, quietly different from my friends, I identified with these characters and their alter egos all through junior school, though my feeling of uniqueness evaporated one afternoon during a History lesson in secondary school, when Malcolm Thomas put his hand up to point out that, actually, Hitler wasn't a German but an Austrian. Knowing it for years but realizing it was a piece of information best kept to myself, I blushed when a couple of boys turned round in their seats to pull faces at me. I tried looking nonchalant, to convey with a raised eyebrow and the curl of my top lip that, yes, I had known all along, and so what, anyway? Fortunately, the nickname

The bo'suns of several vessels eyed Fred suspiciously, dubious that a man with so little facial hair could manage at sea for months at a time without once missing his mother. Despite Fred's protestations, these men shook their heads then turned their backs on the would-be pirate, not realizing how close they had come to inviting trouble aboard their ships.

'*Aber, ich bin* strong,' Fred would shout at their shoulder-blades as they walked up the gangplank and back to their slovenly crews. '*Sehr* strong. *Wirklich.*'

It wasn't until Fred dropped his holdall on the quayside

'Adolf' never caught on with the class, though that evening I renounced my super-hero insignia, insisting my mother remove all the badges of Austrian town-crests she had sewn on the sleeves of my parka.

My fascination with secret identities, I know now, was as much to do with my parents, who represented both halves of the equation, secret identity and super-hero. Dad was mild-mannered Clark Kent, ducking into a telephone box to emerge, an instant later, as Mam, flying into action against truculent shop-assistants or storming into the headmistress's office at the first hint of bullying. She struck fear into pupils and teachers alike. They were head and heart, my parents. My father issued lectures on Marxism – ending arguments with a baffling 'Things are the same, but different' – and was regularly annoyed by films, tutting when a woman who was fleeing from her would-be killer stopped to look back – 'That isn't logical' – or asking where the incidental music was coming from. My mother, on the other hand, would mournfully note the toll life

where *The Jolly Lederhosen* was moored – dinky lipsticks and moisturizers rattling in their rough sacking – that he knew he had found the ship of his destiny, the ship from which revenge could be exacted not just on the Austrian Navy but the whole seagoing world.

'*Ich bin* Fred,' said Fred to a yawning sailor, the only one on deck that balmy afternoon on the outskirts of Graz. 'Master Mariner.'

The sailor was looking after things for his heavy-drinking bo'sun sleeping it off below decks. Fred could hear the gentle sawing of the man's snores even as he was

---

had taken on a cast: who was dead, who was divorced, whose child had died of a drugs overdose.

Despite this, it didn't take my friends long to realize my mother was unquestionably the more formidable of the two, the unpredictable one who could suddenly hurl a teacup at the wall, let fall on my head a pile of comics I had failed to tidy away in the middle of a game, or shake her fist and grit her teeth in a snarl. Even my best friends were wary enough to ration their visits to our house, leaving me to relay her latest exploits, a task I took to with greater satisfaction than my tribulations warranted. Stories of her deeds travelled back to the playground like rumours of the edge of the world, where monsters dwell. In their eyes she became a mythical creature. By the time I was sixteen I was meeting her in combat, pitting my strength against hers, holding back the hand she had raised against me. Aged ten, I had absorbed the lesson that even super-heroes have their weaknesses, be it green kryptonite or one of the Joker's fiendish gizmos.

persuading the daft man to allow him on board, cajoling him, bribing him with a pair of (used) tights for his wife. They were two days at sea and well on the way to Belgium before anyone questioned the presence of the odd man tying ropes to knobs of wood that stuck out on the decks, or shinning up the mast to the crow's nest to look for signs of land.

'Who's that sailor?' the captain asked his dim bo'sun.

'Fred,' whispered the sailor who had invited Fred to join.

'Fred,' replied the bo'sun, not wanting to appear ignorant of what was going on aboard *The Jolly Lederhosen*.

'Fred?' said the captain.

'Fred,' said the bo'sun, growing in confidence. 'A fine addition to the crew.'

'*Sehr gut*,' said the gullible captain, then carried on with his business. His business was stuffing his face with food at every available opportunity, because he was also a greedy captain who had been observed barking orders on the poop deck with a leg of lamb in one hand and a flagon of schnapps in the other, and was once seen raising a *bratwurst* to his eye, mistakenly believing it to be his telescope.

This slovenly man was exactly the sort of fool Fred had hoped to encounter, knowing it wouldn't take much to turn a crew against a captain for whom they had no respect in the first place. Driven irrational by grief,[14] Fred didn't really consider anyone else except herself, and who could blame her.

Below decks, perusing a three-year-old copy of *The Reader's Digest* in his hammock, 'Our *Kapitan*...' Fred would begin a sentence, '*ist*...'

'A fine man,' Fred's companion would say.

'*Ja,*' Fred would reply. '*Ja. Und er* likes his *essen.*'

Fred knew from Heinz's stories that food rations for the average sailor were far inferior to the meals served nightly at the captain's table, where roast potatoes were a regular feature, custard the complement to every dessert, and everything was served on the finest china plates, and

14. In her late seventies, my father's mother, Gladys, alone in her bungalow while my grandfather was in hospital, came to lunch one autumn Sunday and, after a meal I have no recollection of now, fell asleep in the armchair that looked on to our back garden, never to wake. I don't know who first realized that she had died, but our quiet afternoon at home turned quieter, like a world after snow has fallen.

There could have been nothing to see. Nevertheless, aged six, I was ushered upstairs to the boxroom by my brother who, nine years older, understood, and said nothing. While matters were taken care of below, we played with weighty, die-cast Napoleonic soldiers he had painted himself, advancing troops and artillery, rolling the dice, then consulting the rulebook he had bought to find out what happened next.

At first, full of that summer's footage of men on the moon, one giant leap for mankind then the planting of a Stars and Stripes, I had asked to play astronauts. When Karl, too old to

officers ate with solid-silver knives, spoons and forks with intricately carved ivory handles. While the captain was munching on duck, his crew were below, fighting over a maggot someone had discovered in an apple, flipping a doubloon to decide who should have it. This was the lot they had come to expect from life, but Fred (a proto-revolutionary) was determined to show them there was more, that they should look around and see what was going on, to see what they were allowing to take place in the name of the Austrian Admiralty, to see how unfair life was.

Fred would often begin these forays into dissension when the smell of roast meat was wafting down to the crew from the galley directly above their sleeping quarters.

---

lurch around in slow motion, refused, I agreed to his suggestion of war games on the condition that I could be the French because they had all been finished (some with moustaches applied with the finest of brushes), while the British and the Prussians were awaiting detail like gold braid and faces.

'All right,' he said. 'But keep your voice down.'

On the floor that afternoon, as happy to shake a double six as ever, I changed history by winning the battle of Waterloo, a victory I would have shared with my father if, later that day, when everyone had left and I was allowed downstairs, he hadn't turned his face away from us. Holding the mantelpiece ever so gently, he cried. He was so quiet. It was my first sight of grief, and I didn't know what I was supposed to do. My grandmother's chair was empty.

Unlike my father's experience – his father, Bill, died a few months later in hospital, confused by age, unaware that his

This was a design feature no marine architect should have sanctioned, though it would be wrong to castigate anyone for failing to anticipate the talents of Fred for spreading disaffection among simple sailors. Some say that, a hundred years later, the crew of the battleship *Potemkin* were inspired by Fred's sterling work.

The day of the mutiny was probably a Wednesday. The grumbling crew had long since lost track of time, so tormented were they by the smells of cooking that assailed them day and night, provoking more dreams of food than

---

wife's visits had stopped for ever — my mother's grief, four years later, was strung out over months, as first her father and then her mother succumbed to illnesses that took their only daughter back and forth to Austria during 1973 and early 1974, fearful that every meeting would be her last. She flew for the first time in her life and I can recall my father driving her to Heathrow one chilly morning in February with me overdressed in the back seat, excited to be missing school, the *Joe 90* annual I'd been given for Christmas open on my lap until I was car-sick.

'Are we there yet?' I asked every few miles.

The floors of the terminal were icily dazzling. I had seen nothing like them and made a nuisance of myself, a little Narcissus, staring down to catch my reflection as we bustled around, checking-in my mother's cases then seeing her to the departure lounge where she was too sad to be sad about leaving us. Though a growing nine-year-old, I still craned my neck to look up at her, but that day she seemed shrunken, more round-shouldered than I was ever allowed to be, a black astrakhan coat loose around her. A coat of worms.

fantasies of their wives back home. Some dreamt of both; huge sides of bacon dressed in dirndls gambolling through sunlit meadows humming tunes from *The Sound of Music*. There is no way of knowing now if it was a Wednesday, for the logbook that recorded the first moments of the mutiny was lost overboard in the fighting that raged on into the evening, until control of the ship was in the recently hardened hands of Fred.

What happened next was the first example of Fred the Unspeakable's legendary generosity. Rather than making

---

'Don't be any trouble,' she muttered, stooping to kiss me. She had already forgotten I didn't like to be kissed any more.

In recompense, after we had watched the flight take off, my father gave me five pence to buy a Marvel comic I'd spotted in the enormous shop on the concourse. It was *Journey into the Unknown*, the only edition of that title I ever saw. There was a beefy robot on the cover being lowered on pulleys as two awestruck scientists gazed up at their amazing creation. I stored it with the rest of my collection, in a plastic bag under the boxroom bed, though I never told my father what a disappointing read it was, that the artwork was nothing like as good as the figures drawn by my favourite artist, Neal Adams, whose super-heroes looked more realistic than anyone else's.

My mother left again that July, a few weeks after my tenth birthday, before school had even broken up for the summer. This time I moaned about missing Sports Day – I was down for the long jump – and asked to stay with neighbours after school. Distracted, they didn't take me seriously and, sulking all the way up in the car, I ostentatiously stared out of the window

their fat captain walk the plank — in their mutinous talk below deck in the nights leading up to the coup, sailors had placed wagers on the distance along the strip of wood the captain would walk before it snapped under his weight — Fred set him adrift in an open boat with two oars and enough food to last for a week. Enough food for an ordi-

---

whenever spoken to, convinced I would never be reprimanded for rudeness when Life had broken free of its ropes to slip and slide unpredictably, like cargo in a ship's hold. The flat, ugly landscape sped by, as grey as it was green, and even the thought of my father's chip butties didn't cheer me up.

A month later, the day after her muted return, I was playing on my own in our back garden, fishing an Action-Man out of the tin drum filled with murky rainwater that stood outside our greenhouse. Pretending he was Count Otto, one of the Austrian Navy's most renowned sons, I had trussed him with fuse-wire then weighed him down with stones, sinking him into the darkness the day after my mother had caught her flight home to her parents.

(During 1973 I came to consider Austria her real home, an impression she did nothing to discourage, her groaned 'I should never have left' or 'Why did I come here?' always loud enough for my father and me to hear. I had seen and read enough science fiction to know that if you alter the past, events in the present — who lives and who dies, who is and isn't born — are bound to change, so I wondered if she was wishing me out of existence, and if so, why. I buried this nugget of logic for years, resurrecting it during the fights we began to have when I was tall enough to answer her back.

Humming the opening bars of *Thus Spake Zarathustra*, then

nary man, that is, but for the captain, who could guess. It was something else for the crew to bet about, though they knew they would never learn of their captain's fate.

'Curse you, Mister Fred,' the disgruntled man bellowed.

[This was my father's chance to do his Charles Laughton, a performance I didn't fully appreciate until I saw the actor as Captain Bligh on TV one Saturday afternoon at University.]

---

switching to a David Bowie number parodied by my father as he climbed the stairs on school mornings –

> 'Ground Control to Major Tom,
> I hope you've got your trousers on . . .'

– I salvaged my Action-Man from his watery grave. A sorry state, he rose dripping from the stagnant water, his limbs twisted at grotesque angles, his joints rusted, his clothes green and smelly.

A ruined thing.

At ten, and still afraid of my mother, I had fretted that she might ask me where the doll was and, too scared of her wrath to lie, I would have to own up to my vandalism. The previous day, the day she returned, I had been crouching by the goldfish pond looking for signs of life in the weed-choked waters, poking the snails that clung to the slimy sides just below the surface, when my bedroom window swung open with a shudder and comics began flying out like pigeons startled from a coop, fluttering feebly to the ground like Hermann the Birdman.

'I told you to put your things away!' my mother bellowed from inside the room, loud enough for the neighbourhood to hear.

I abandoned the snail hunt at once, running to where my

'Curse you!'

The crew, though not Fred, roared with laughter, throwing their heads back like over-enthusiastic extras in a Hollywood epic.

'Ha, ha, ha,' they crowed. *Auf Wiedersehen*, Captain Fatty!'

---

comics rained, stooping to discover which ones had come loose from their staples, which ones were torn. I couldn't say if my mother had known, but many turned out to be my favourites: first editions of *Kamandi* (The Last Boy on Earth) and *Swamp Thing*, *Batman* 237 – the battle against Two-Face which opened in the rigging of a four-masted ship that reminded me of my father's stories – and *Green Lantern* 76, which was not only worth more than the shilling paid for it two years earlier but had my favourite super-hero's motto of that summer, 'In Brightest Day and Blackest Night No Evil Shall Escape My Sight.' I knew things in Austria were serious but, until I knelt before that pile of wrecked comics, I hadn't understood how serious.

Now, a day later, the horrible doll was in my hands and it was useless. Hoping she wouldn't notice its absence from my cupboard under the stairs, I decided to be tidier with my things at least until the business with Austria had passed. As I towelled it dry with an old pair of my father's Y-fronts borrowed from his toolbox (my mother insisted he recycle them as rags), a rotten spring snapped and an arm fell off.

'I'm going to the super*markt*.'

Awed by the destruction wrought on the Christmas present in my paws, I hadn't heard my mother stomping downstairs, and turned too quickly, the rag and the Action-Man at my side, guilt leaking from my wide-eyed face. Preoccupied with the

'But we won't be *seeing* you *again*, will we? Ha, ha, ha . . .'

[This is how my father taught me a little German, even though he could scarcely speak a word himself.]

The seven years that followed were less a reign of terror than a series of humiliating setbacks for the Austrian Navy, their endeavours to protect merchant vessels hounded by

---

grief growing inside her like a terrible vegetable, she noticed neither my face nor my hands.

'You stay in the house,' she said, taking her purse from beside the telephone, 'and don't touch anything. I won't be long.'

It was a close call, but I didn't dwell on it. This was my chance, I thought, as the door slammed, leaving the house still as a desert planet even wind had forsaken. Dust sailed on a ray of light that shone into the front room like a laser beam. My father was at work, balancing the books for British Steel, and I was alone, free to explore.

'To boldly go,' I said aloud, 'where no man has gone before!' then raced upstairs and into my parents' bedroom, pausing only to fling the useless Action-Man into my toy cupboard.

Though I knew a sadness had overwhelmed my powerful mother, I was still surprised when she didn't hand me a gift at Arrivals the day before. After all, her last trip had yielded a set of coloured pencils. So, like a good detective, I deduced that she'd either left my present in her suitcase or, sad to the point of amnesia, put it to one side while she was unpacking. The first place to look was under the bed, where my parents always slid one of the suitcases when it was done with, where the air was stale, where objects became furry with neglect. Flat on my stomach, I explored the strange new world, seeking out new life and new civilizations, pointing the feeble beam of my

Fred the Unspeakable and his crew of cutthroats invariably failing. 'Cutthroats' was the Admiralty's description of the genial sailors loyal to Fred. They also coined the nickname 'Unspeakable' in the WANTED posters they stuck to fir trees across the Gulf of Austria.

---

torch into the corner where the bed met the bedside table, the top of my head brushing the hessian underside, breathing softly so as not to disturb the dust. One of the two suitcases was there, unpromisingly concave, but I pulled it out anyway, just as the batteries of my torch gave up the ghost and the filament of the tiny bulb cooled.

Nothing inside but a sheet of rumpled tissue-paper.

I was momentarily disheartened. Convinced the smaller case was the hidey-hole, I turned my attention to the wardrobe, where I knew they stored the fatter of the two pieces of luggage, the one they considered their best, the one good enough for funerals and weddings, if that had been what you took to those occasions. (There were others in the loft, scratched, enormous coffins I climbed inside when I was eight, but those had only been brought out when we all went away, my brother included.) The wardrobe doors concertinaed open and a smell of mothballs wafted out. On tiptoe—my father needed a chair, my mother nothing—I stretched like Eve for the handle of the leather case overhanging the top shelf, nestled beside two floppy-brimmed hats I hadn't seen my mother wearing since the 1960s.

'Give me . . . your hand, Scotty,' I squeaked, my impersonation of William Shatner no more than an American accent, and then, 'I cannae do it, Cap'n.'

Short by no more than six months of growth, half a fingertip – I was a Mödritscher in the making – I lost my footing with the

116

The pirates heaped humiliations on the heads of sailors unfortunate enough to get in their way, making them wear girdles, skirts and brassières or keep babies' dummies in their mouths, which is how they would be found when they were eventually rescued by their compatriots. The

---

prize in my right hand, toppling to the double bed, the suitcase flapping open, disgorging a pair of my mother's flag-sized knickers, a box of paper tissues, and a brown-paper parcel which flew further than the rest, bouncing off the squashy headboard behind me.

'Holy underwear, Batman!'

I lay there for ages, like a stuntman, wishing I had my friend John with me to share the joke, rehearsing my description of the scene for the first day of term in September – '. . . and I nearly cracked my head open on the bedpost . . .' (there was no bedpost) – when I heard music.

Muffled, tortuously slow, the melancholy tune was coming from the package. I was sure this had to be my present awaiting colourful wrapping-paper, so there was nothing else to do but unwrap it, even though I guessed that resealing it exactly as it was could prove tricky, not to mention the look of surprise I would have to fake when it was eventually given to me. The music box, for that's what it was, continued playing while I gently unfolded the paper as if in the middle of a decorous game of Pass the Parcel. The tune, my mother told me years later, was the 'Erzherzog Johann', a mournful air that grew even sadder as the mechanism wound down and the music ground to a halt. It was like the promise of ice-cream sold by depressives.

Before I was born, Oma travelled to Wales on her own to spend a month with my parents. One evening, she went to the

pirates left behind carefully written notes taunting the Navy for their hopeless attempts to stop piracy in their own backyard. Once, for the safe return of a Viennese captain kidnapped from a ship off the coast of Switzerland

---

Mermaid overlooking Swansea Bay, for some reason without my mother, who was told later that Oma had sung that music-box tune in the pub,

> *'Wo ich geh und steh*
> *Tuat mir mein Herz so weh,'*

and that, when she'd finished, everyone in the bar applauded.

I worked slowly, like a bomb-disposal expert. By the time it had been unwrapped, the music was over. An Austrian chalet with a water-wheel that turned when the key was wound, it was occupied by a tiny couple joined by one piece of wire. They emerged in turns, like weather people, when a knob on the roof was twisted. It didn't take me long to recognize it as the one I had seen on display in Uncle Günther's house the previous summer, the one his mother, my Oma, had given to him for his birthday. Why he would have given it to my mother for me I couldn't begin to understand. It wasn't the best present in the world, I thought, the pencils were better, but with the world turned upside down in recent months – my mother missing work and going on aeroplanes, for starters – I knew gratitude was the wisest response. I only hoped that I was a better actor than my father and surprise could be counterfeited.

'What the hell is this?'

My father was standing in the doorway with his shoes in his hand. (My mother insisted on socks or slippers upstairs.) He was almost as alarmed as I was.

'I wasn't feeling well,' was all I could think to say.

and imprisoned for a month, Fred demanded that one of their taunting letters be published in newspapers far and wide. The text was the cause of much gossip for years afterwards, and the Austrian Empire was never considered quite as foolproof again.

'Get out of here. At once.' His voice was stern, but he never shouted. 'What do you think you're playing at?'

'. . . and I lost my torch.'

Even as I heard myself offering the worst excuse ever invented by someone in a fix, I thanked God that it was my father catching me. There was a hole in his brown socks. My mother would have mended that in better times.

'I'm sorry . . . I thought it was for me.'

For a moment, the sight of Günther's music box seemed to scare him, though I didn't see how that could be possible, It was only a music box, and I had been very careful unwrapping it. He couldn't have seen it hitting the headboard, that was for sure; and anyway, the music came out despite the bashing it took.

That night, awake in bed, I listened to my parents arguing in the living room, their voices muffled by the ceiling and the carpets. This wasn't the first or the last occasion when I would hear their voices raised so violently, though this time I knew what it was about. The fact that I was the cause of their anger kept me awake in the dark for hours. Staring at the faces in my curtains, gargoyles the street-lamp in the lane illuminated so gruesomely, I worried about my mother's transgression, imagining my fierce uncle's face, his terrible expression as he stood before the spot where his music box had been. I fell asleep thinking of the shelf where he had placed it, as empty now as the plinth for the Baron's ice statue in the depths of August.

Dear Idiots of the Austrian Admiralty,
Your feeble attempts to stop our reign over the
Seven Seas and sail wheresoever we please
demonstrates to your enemies at home and
abroad how silly you really are, how sly
and how many sweet men have lost their lives
due to your unpleasant ways.

Yours sincerely,

The Free Fred Navy

It was only after the wife of the hapless captain held by Fred and the pirates had pleaded to the Austrian Emperor to agree to the terms that the letter was printed on the front page of every newspaper in Europe, much to the monarch's head-shaking dismay. Some editors went so far as to issue cartoons of the pirates, with Fred looming tall and broad at their head, a puny Austrian rating cowering at their feet, and one scurvy-looking chap merrily chomping on the globe, like the etchings of Napoleon carving up the world with a knife and fork that did the rounds a few years later.

After that, Fred's progress was faithfully reported around the world, articles were written by journalists who considered Fred a hero, and a number of cartoons were advanced as the true likeness of a pirate many had seen but few described in any credible detail. The one that showed the great pirate with an enormous, shovel-shaped beard amused Fred in particular and the drawing found pride of place in Fred's mournful, underlit cabin,[15] pinned above the table where Fred dined and (more importantly) washed alone.

'Merchantman ahoy!' the cry came one afternoon in the straits of Belgium, while Fred was below, nostalgically examining the bundle of lipsticks, dresses and powder puffs brought from home all those years before, recalling the good old days. 'One frigate with her!'

Used to the routine by now, the pirates of *The Jolly Lederhosen* hoisted the Jolly Roger and put their cutlasses between their teeth, an exercise which, even after years of practice, still made them dribble down their hooped shirts.

'Aaar! Aaar! Ha-Aaar!' they growled together, preparing themselves.

---

15. Elfrieda's sad cabin came to mind when, after twenty years, I revisited number 50 *Floßländ*, Hari's warrenous bungalow on the outskirts of Knittelfeld, while he was away in former Yugoslavia, north of the battlefields, on a cigarette-run with Gerda. Too old to chase around the countryside every day, my mother decided we should spend an afternoon sunbathing, reading, or weeding the garden. In the hour before lunch, I drifted from room to room.

The place had gone to seed since Lisa's death. Scruffy as a Santa's Grotto in Woolworths, its small windows were hidden by fat curtains permanently drawn against the sun. With shutters and net curtains, *im Falle des Falles*, electric light was needed all day, even by the artificial monstera, ferns and rubber plants in their gravel bed beneath lights rigged to a timer. My

[My father was a great pirate growler.]

'Easy pickings, Cap'n!' the bo'sun (now one of Fred's most fervent supporters) growled happily when his captain appeared, a blusher brush crushed in his fist.

Little did the pirates know that the seemingly ill-equipped frigate and the meek vessel under its protection (*The Gypsy Moth*) were in fact a trap set by the Austrian Navy to capture once and for all the menace of the High Seas that had plagued them for seven years. Aboard the merchant ship, promoted for his years of cruelty to Vice Admiral, and sporting a bushy beard not unlike the one cartoonists around the world had attributed to Fred, a sailor turned to face *The Jolly Lederhosen*, his glass eye glinting

---

uncle hadn't bothered to deactivate the system after substituting the real for the phoney. The whole house was textured, even the bathroom, where a denture plate of six teeth soaked in cloudy water above a sink girdled with dirt. Furry, almost breathing, the décor was so unlike Günther's that it was impossible to recognize their two places as the creations of brothers. A dirty, cream-coloured pelt, like a sheepskin rug, hung on the wall above the sofa. On the sofa's greying, fleecy cover, a ghoulish doll slumped to one side, its eyes wide open, staring at a dining table littered with Gameboys belonging to Hari's grandsons, away with him and Gerda. Among the toys was a hollow, triangular cardboard flytrap with a little cairn of flies at its heart. In the twilit living room, side by side, two armchairs faced the television, one a brown-corduroy-and-chrome beast that reclined, lifting the sitter's feet off the ground like a dental patient's, the other balding on both arms.

in the sunlight as he did. A nasty-looking shrunken man stood one pace behind him.

[The first time my father told this tale, he stopped to study my face, asking if I knew who the sinister men on deck were. 'Of course I know,' I said.]

'Ready to boar –'

Before the bo'sun could finish his sentence, the two ships opened fire, blowing off the main mast of *The Jolly Lederhosen*, thus preventing any escape. Not that Fred and the crew would have countenanced such action, they would never have lived it down. Their blades between their teeth, they swung on ropes back and forth like conkers, from ship to ship, knocking against each other

---

Even during the years when my parents stayed with Günther, my father took to sitting there in the afternoons, watching old episodes of *Star Trek* dubbed into German. He must have brightened up markedly on days when he recognized a particular scene, knowing at last what was going on. Whenever they telephoned from Austria and my mother put him on the line, he would run through the plot of that day's adventure, looking to me to bridge the gaps in his understanding, believing I still cared.

'I have no idea,' I would say. '*You* were watching.'

Smaller than I'd remembered, the house had been divided in two for Lisa's parents but, since her death and their return to Vienna, the other half was occupied by a young family for a peppercorn rent. Part of the couple's side of the bargain, my mother complained to me that afternoon as she unwound the hose to water the flowerbed, was to cut the grass and water

until one sailor would fall into the sea, then surface, spluttering.

[My father assured me that all sailors could swim.]

'Cap'n! It's a trap, Cap'n. Run for it,' the cabin boy shouted, swinging from a rope and having more fun than was appropriate.

'Never,' boomed Fred. 'Courage, my lads!'

The boldest of all pirates, Fred picked up a cannon

———————

the plants in the garden. They were also told to keep the two seven-year-old boys on their side of the house, though that was proving impossible to enforce. The day we were there, the bolder of the two lurked at the front gate, hiding from his brother who was maintaining his search in their half of the garden, trusting his sibling had stuck to the rules. From time to time, my father tried reprimanding them, though his voice was too quiet to be a deterrent. Besides, they knew no English. It was up to my mother to glower in a manner familiar from my own childhood. She hadn't lost her touch. Meekly, the boy hiding slunk away. There was a joyful yelp as his brother discovered him.

I left the house to find my father on the garden swing, struggling with a crossword. Dressed in a sky-blue, short-sleeved shirt and beige slacks, he was sporting a pair of futuristic, wrap-around sunglasses so big that they fitted over his bifocals. They made him look blind.

'I'm surprised someone with your education couldn't finish this,' he said.

'I didn't try.'

'*Ruin*. Something, something, C, something, something. Five letters.'

and tucked it under one arm, lighting it with a cigar then aiming it at the hull of the frigate.

KA-BOOM!

The recoil scarcely troubled, Fred, who, scooping another cannonball from the deck, reloaded the heavy gun. Then, ugly as sin, the figure of one-eyed Rolf appeared before Fred, his unblinking eye fixing the pirate captain. Fred knew at once who it was. Heinz's letters had spoken

---

I bent over to look at the two-day-old copy of the *Daily Express* handed out on the flight over.

'*Decay*. Promise to bury someone is *undertake*.'

From the number of empty boxes it was clear he wasn't doing very well, though I didn't want to sit anywhere near the three grimy pillows beside him, primary-coloured like a child's building blocks but matted like the skin hanging above the sofa. My mother emerged with sandwiches and drinks, laying the table that Hari had placed in the garden under a white canopy. It was the latest trend in Austria, eating undercover alfresco. Small, fussy wasps had congregated in its roof and I wondered, as I nibbled a *bratwurst* sandwich in a silence punctuated by the clicking of cutlery and their low moaning, my head tilted back for fear of an attack, if our lunch would bring them down on us. They passed the time thumping their heads against the canvas ceiling, though I couldn't work out if they were trapped or liked it up there. Halving a bread roll in the palm of his hand, my father nicked the skin between his thumb and forefinger.

'Jesus!'

He bled more than I would have expected, staunching the cut with a paper tissue until my mother ordered him to leave the table because there was still food present.

all about the cruel, dead-eyed captain and now here he was, after seven years, an easy target for someone as strong as Fred with half as good an aim.

To the amazement of everyone that could see, Fred pulled off his hat and a coil of blonde hair tumbled from the tricorn. With two quick swipes of the lipstick, a couple of strokes of the blusher brush then a fluent sweep

---

'He's doing that more and more,' she said when he'd ambled inside.

Ants struggling up blades of grass. Flies negotiating the boulders of food on the tablecloth. Wasps drowsing. It was August, in the middle of the afternoon in the middle of Europe and no one was moving. Once in a while, a car drove past the hedge that shielded Hari's garden from the road, racing nothing.

After returning to finish lunch, my father disappeared to watch television while my mother, unable to sit quietly for long, stripped down to her huge brassière and white shorts to begin weeding and watering the vegetable patch. She cursed Hari's idle tenants while simultaneously enjoying the fact that there was something to occupy her afternoon. Her huge shadow plunged flowerbeds into darkness in the middle of the day. Now and then, she straightened up, her face flushed, her forehead beaded, muttering that the young couple's rent was overdue or wondering what exactly it was that Gerda did to justify her place in Hari's affections. I played with the hose, pressing my thumb on the nozzle to send a peacock's tail of water pattering on leaves that hadn't felt rain in weeks, directing a jet at the base of a pink hydrangea, watching the water puddle, killing it with kindness.

of a comb through her locks, Fred was at last revealed as Elfrieda. Overhead, swinging from the masts, the crew gasped as one, momentarily forgetting they were in the middle of a battle.

'Remember Heinz Vogel!' Elfrieda shouted, then lit the fuse with her cigar. *Nicht vergessen.*

KA-BOOM!

'Come and look at this, Steve.'

My father was at the window, holding the heavy curtains apart with one hand and beckoning me with the other.

Inside, widening my eyes to adjust to the murk, I found him on the corduroy chair in front of the television. I stood in the doorway for a moment, expecting him to say something. He continued to hang on every word, every mismatched movement of the lips, his eyes unblinking.

'Have you watched this at Günther's?'

'Not yet,' I mumbled. 'That looks nasty. Does it hurt?'

He was holding a blood-stained Kleenex and the skin where he had cut himself was a rich purple.

'Nah,' he said.

Having fetched me inside to share this common interest, however, my father was unable to look away from the set long enough to talk.

'Square eyeballs,' I said.

– His small, blue irises; the whites of his eyes; the red mark on the bridge of his nose where his spectacles had rested; the top of his head protected with sun-cream . . . I was about to go when he called me back.

'Is this the one where the monster lays its eggs in the tunnel?'

With a great puff of smoke, the cannon beneath her arm erupted like a volcano and, quicker than the human eye could follow, the ball flew to its target, striking it with an almighty crack.

'Nicht vergessen.'

The deck where Rolf and Wolfgang had been standing fell in a shower of splinters pattering like hail around the sailors of the Austrian Navy, a glass eye spinning on the

---

The screen was filled with talking heads. There were no laser beams, no dematerializations to entertain a monoglot, nothing to explain what was happening. I might have appeared to be following the plot, but I was comparing what was on screen with memories of various episodes; the turn of a head, the configuration of people on an under-furnished set, the close-up of a worried face.

'She's still digging,' I said.

His eyes held by the flickering images, 'You must understand,' he said, 'your mother is a sick woman.'

Perhaps I was supposed to sit and watch it with him, in the chair with the balding arms, but even in English this was never one of my favourite stories. I drifted away and he didn't even notice, first to a photograph on the mantelpiece of Hari, Lisa and Lianne – a picture from the 1960s, to judge from their ages and clothing – then, wincing, out into the light, a car zooming past as if to emphasize how quiet it was; so quiet that I could hear the trapped wasps fizzing and my mother digging in Hari's vegetable plot, pulling up weeds that were halfway to choking everything.

I could hear them tearing.

spot. Men of both sides turned to where Elfrieda had been standing a moment before, but she had vanished as thoroughly as the two villains. Only a cerise lipstick rolling down the tilting deck remained.

Men stood, their mouths agape, unable to believe what they had seen, that Fred was a woman — a woman, moreover, who had disappeared before their eyes.

Unfortunately for the pirates, their enemy was first to recover from the shock and, before they knew what was happening, they found themselves led below the deck of the battered frigate, prisoners of the Austrian Empire, *The Jolly Lederhosen* towed forlornly behind them as they sailed to Vienna, their once-proud ship's sails in shreds.

Some say Elfrieda escaped overboard with the key to a treasure chest buried on a remote island somewhere in the Gulf of Austria, the sort of place that has a single Christmas tree tall in the middle of a heap of sand. No one could prove this, of course, but when the members of Elfrieda's crew were eventually released by the authorities (who could do no less, when the papers welcomed them home as heroes), each man discovered a substantial amount of money had been deposited in his bank account. More than enough to settle down and live a decent life.

It was the least Elfrieda's men deserved. The chance of a fresh start, a reward for years of loyalty. For not one of them mentioned, not even to one another when drunk and reminiscing, the figurehead of an Amazonian woman they had all spied on the once-bare prow of *The Jolly Lederhosen*. As they disembarked in chains that brilliant November morning in 1799, shivering in the cold air, the faintest of smiles flickered on that figurehead's lips.

5.

STEFAN

The tale of Stefan, cabin-boy of the *Sousaphone*, the first submarine in the service of the Austrian Navy, and how that vessel wound up in the branches of a sycamore in New Jersey [or 'Noo Joyzee', as my father used to say in his best boxing-referee's voice],[16] was one of his most puzzling bedtime stories. Puzzling because of its aimlessness, and the feeling I had, sunk in the pillow, my eyelids

16. Even now, I cannot reconcile my father's communist politics with his enthusiasm for James Bond films, nor his innate gentleness with the pleasure he derived from boxing. He relished the films for their gadgets, their colour and relentless action, the way cars and villains were trashed with equal insouciance (even though the baddies were generally Reds). His love of boxing was, in actual fact, a love of Muhammad Ali.

I don't know when my father first became aware of the Louisville Lip. If it wasn't the boxer's gold-medal-winning performance at the Olympics when he was still Cassius Clay then it must have been his conversion to the Nation of Islam, his refusal to go to Vietnam, and the subsequent stripping of his heavyweight title in 1967. He delighted as much in Ali's poetic arrogance outside the ring, his 'Float like a butterfly, sting like a bee' or 'I AM the Greatest!', as he did in his footwork inside it.

drooping, that, of all his tales, it was the one least in a hurry to reach its destination, that my father was prolonging it with elaborate descriptions of an undersea world both beautiful and threatening, a world he didn't want to leave.

On the edge of the bed, leaning forward as if to peer into the darkness, his hands denting the duvet, he conducted me through the valleys of coral mountains, past shipwrecks buried in the sand, over crops of seaweed swaying in the currents. Fish performed fluid acrobatics around the submarine's conning tower, the periscope a

---

My father was primarily an armchair enthusiast, in front of the telly for the Rumble in the Jungle and the Thrilla in Manila, and I went along with this, sitting beside him on the sofa, until the mid 1970s. In my second term at Penlan Comprehensive, tall for my age, I was beaten up on the way home one afternoon, on waste ground, by an older boy who pushed, kicked and butted me above my right eye. He had to jump to make contact, even though he was a few years older, and I was left with an egg-sized lump on my left eyebrow that bloomed, over-night, into a huge, purple shiner. Boxing, James Bond, and all glorifications of violence lost their appeal, and I became withdrawn, the beginning of my adolescent sulky years, when my parents didn't know how to talk to me and I didn't want to talk to them.

Around the same time, when their marriage was at its glass-jawed frailest, my father attended a couple of local boxing matches, dragging my mother along for the boozy gatherings if not the action. It all began when my father did a photographic job for Eddie Richards, a sometime promoter who wanted his

lightning conductor; shoals of sudden light, there momentarily then gone.

The only child of a poor family from a village so small
that no one bothered with surnames, a place that even
the most detailed maps of Austria failed to record, Stefan
had always dreamt of going to sea.

Born the year Queen Victoria died, he grew to boyhood
with the smell of the ocean in his lungs, a gale in his hair,
his eyes in love with blue horizons, though mountains
obscured his view of the distance.

---

collection of cigarette cards of legendary boxers blown up and
mounted on his office wall. Laying the cards on the swirly
living-room carpet, beneath the tripod, Dad photographed
them one summer, then, using Velindre Camera Club's darkroom, produced versions of Rocky Marciano and Joe Louis
more ill-defined but taller than him. In return, he was handed
tickets to a couple of bouts, the kind of matches so lacking in
grace that my parents must have wondered, as they looked
owlishly up at the ring from their seats in the third row,
why on earth they had turned out to watch two men beating
the crap out of one another with so little finesse, their ugly
couplings on the bruised canvas a parody of the last dance
of the night.

Aged eleven, I was old enough to be left alone on their
evenings out, a little afraid of the dark even then, though I
never admitted it. The sounds of our home's timbers creaking
as I lay awake in bed were as good as monsters stirring, the
way the breeze from an open window rippled my heavy bedroom
curtains tantamount to an invasion, the glass door in the

A bright lad, he was near the top in every subject taught in the one-roomed village school, Maths and Physics included, though he eventually became bored of addition, subtraction and long division. The only Science lesson he could summon up any enthusiasm for was the one in which the teacher, Mrs Green, dropped a stone in a bucket of water and talked about the ripples. An enjoyable enough experiment, it was one he could watch only so often

---

hall singing in a high wind. To block the noises out, I played my brother's recordings of the Top Twenty on the reel-to-reel he left when he went to university. Otis Redding, Wilson Pickett, Smokey Robinson, the spools turning, the machine's pale-green light barely scratching the darkness. Listening for my parents, determined to see them safely home, I usually fell asleep only to be woken by my mother bending to kiss me goodnight as my father switched the tape recorder off, the end of the tape flapping as the full reel turned fruitlessly.

I wished I had slept through the night they returned from the second bout they'd attended in 1975. My mother arrived first, at one in the morning, ten minutes ahead of my father, banging the door so loudly that the commotion invaded my dreams, her slurred muttering eventually waking me. That night, I had decided against the tape recorder, so her voice was carrying from the hall to my pillow too clearly to ignore.

'Bastard . . . Bastard . . . Bastard . . .'

I crept downstairs in my Kung Fu pyjamas without switching any lights on. Moonlight soldered the stairs, the paint of the banister sparkled. Familiar with the sight of my mother pissed, in mourning for her parents, her eyes swollen, her face wrecked

without yawning, widening his eyes every now and then to make a startled look, his desperate attempt to stay awake.

'I'm resting my eyes,' he said one afternoon, when Mrs Green, bucket in hand, asked him what on earth he thought he was doing. 'Resting my eyes for Art.'

His favourite subject, Art was the only lesson never to send him to sleep. Stefan loved to draw, and did so

---

by tears, I was dreading the worst. Flapping like a hopeless mime, she was in the kitchen, staggering, sobbing and swearing in the half-light.

'Bloody thing . . . Bloody bastarding thing,' then, faintly, like a broken doll, 'Mamma . . .'

'Be quiet,' I whispered, praying the neighbours wouldn't hear, thankful she wasn't howling.

'. . .'s nothing to eat.'

Her face in shadow, she was holding a handkerchief to her crown as she thumped the cooker. It rattled, the grill-door dropping open as she turned away into a column of moonlight. One of my late grandmother's (her initials, *CM*, embroidered in a corner), the handkerchief was soaked with blood, thick blobs, thicker than a nosebleed's, and I could see, even as she lurched in front of me, unable to focus, unable to tell who I was, that the hair on the back of her head was sticky, matted, blood oozing from her skull.

'What the hell is going on?'

I didn't know what to do so I started shouting at her, shouting and sobbing. I can't remember everything I said, nor how angry my tears were. I was outraged at being scared, mortified to see an adult sloshed, afraid my mother might

whenever he could, with coloured pencils or charcoal sticks, drawing from life — the mountains above the village, an ancient relative, the family goat — or drawing from his imagination — huge battleships in stormy seas, gulls

---

die before my eyes and I wouldn't know who to call for help.

'What the hell is going on?' I repeated, sounding more like my father than I realized at the time. 'Where's Dad?'

She swung an arm to swat me, but there was no real danger of her landing a blow. I had seen enough of her drunk and enraged not to be too troubled by her hands. Blood was the frightening development.

She reeled away, heading for the bathroom, clambering upstairs on all fours as my father arrived, his key bouncing off the lock until it eventually found the hole.

Even with all his hours in front of the television watching Muhammad Ali floor opponents without them laying a glove on him, I couldn't believe my flyweight father had learnt enough to be able to flatten my all-conquering mother.

'Is she here?' my father asked, his voice slurred. I could tell he wasn't as pissed as my mother. 'Bloody woman. Bloody stupid woman. Drinking with tablets when she knows she shouldn't.'

(My mother had been prescribed Valium six months earlier, but, against her doctor's advice, had continued drinking.)

Wiping my eyes in my sleeves, angrier still, I could see that my father's nose was bulbous as a clown's. He, too, held a bloody handkerchief in front of his face, fumbling the keys back into his pocket.

'Jesus Christ . . .' He was looking at the crumpled rag in his fist, perhaps for the first time, realizing how much blood he

battered by a force-nine gale, fearsome pirates with scars on their cheeks, bulging storm-clouds over granite waves. He even drew the ripples in the Physics-lesson bucket like the wrinkles on his Opa's face.

---

had lost. 'Bloody stupid woman. I don't know what's the matter with her.'

I had already accused them of drifting in with the wrong crowd, drinking with Swansea mobsters (the Taffia), shady underworld types who were leading them astray, whisky by whisky, and here was the proof, the tap running in the bathroom and my father, on the bottom step, dabbing his nose, inadvertently blocking my path upstairs. I left him there, bewildered and muttering. My feet freezing, I curled up on the sofa and tried to sleep.

A similar episode occurred the previous December, when my father returned home alone from a party in the early hours of Christmas Eve. She turned up well into the morning, smelling of drink and with a look on her face that might have been sheepishness, though I had never seen its like before. They traded accusations until my mother slapped my father across the face, a blow that sent him hurtling across the bed. By then, everything had gone to pieces in our lives, so much so that none of the food shopping for Christmas had been done, a fact I found inexplicable, a sign of how things had deteriorated. That afternoon I trailed around town with my mother, praying, as we drove into the centre, that she wouldn't be breathalysed then thrown into jail for New Year. All the while she said she had nothing left, and even, in the middle of one shop, asked me what the point in living was.

'Not here,' I muttered. 'Not here . . . Please.'

For the first time, I could see her bulk had been hollowed by

139

'I think I should be going now,' he had announced one day, aged three.

His parents always teased him about this precocious desire to travel, to be away from them, as they teased him about his yearning for a pair of pointy shoes.

By the time he was thirteen, however, they came to understand that Stefan would leave home sooner rather than later, his wanderlust more than a phase that other children abandon when they discover the scent of the girl at the desk in front, or see afresh the blond hair of the boy they used to call 'Smelly' lit like a halo.

One afternoon soon after his fateful birthday, Stefan

---

grief, her eyes sunken, her skin grainy and white, lacking its usual tan. Though still a giant, she was half her normal size.

'I shouldn't have come here,' she murmured as I disappeared down the tinned-soup aisle, looking for a box of crackers. 'This country.'

She steered our trolley around the supermarket, so unenthusiastic about the day's itinerary that I didn't even ask to push the thing. She was taking items from the shelf without even studying the labels, sage-and-onion stuffing, tangerines, peanuts, cranberry sauce, chocolates; her desultory shopping a portent that life would never be the same again.

Even with all the blood, the post-boxing-match episode was nothing in comparison, and became a trivial incident as soon as I'd ascertained that the wound on my mother's head was not only minor but wasn't even inflicted by my father. It was a result of her tripping drunkenly on the way out of the arena and hitting her head on the kerb. Nor was my father's bloody

was alone, sitting a mile from the village, a drawing of a mountain rising up like a tidal wave at his feet, beside the perfect mirror of a lake he broke every now and then with stones thrown the length of two cricket pitches.

[They don't play cricket in Austria, my father explained, not wanting to confuse me; no fielders slapping their thighs in the slips, no yodelled 'Howzat!']

Gossip of strange goings-on in the area had followed a rash of unsettling portents: eerie groanings after dark, dead fish floating on the lake's placid surface. This alerted villagers to the peril of allowing their children to wander off alone. However, Stefan had decided to use that Friday after school to visit his favourite spot, taking with him his

---

nose given to him by his enraged wife. A passing taxi-driver, on seeing my father bent over my injured mother (haranguing her as she lay in a heap on the pavement), assumed my father had been assaulting her, stopped his cab in the middle of the road, thumped my hapless father, then gave my injured mother a lift home. My dad was left in the gutter my mother had occupied five minutes earlier. Fitting retribution, the driver must have thought.

My father never went to another bout, though his love of Muhammad Ali continued even after the boxer's career was ended by age and Parkinson's, his looks intact. 'He could box, eh?'

Comparing photos of my father taken before and after this incident, however, it's possible to see that his nose was never the same.

sketchbook and a handful of coloured pencils sharpened so often they were, by then, no bigger than a toddler's fingers. Splinters of ice thickening at the water's edge, it was a dazzling, cloudless afternoon at the very end of his childhood.

'Thar she blows,' he murmured under his breath, unwilling to disturb the snow-capped mountains, when the arc of each stone was completed by a plume of water rising in the distance. The faraway *plop* echoed minutely in the still air. 'Man the harpoons.'

He had never read Herman Melville but knew all about the monstrous whale and the one-legged man who pursued it across the Seven Seas, driven to distraction by revenge.

Then, with the little cairn of pebbles gathered on his walk to the lake almost exhausted and his things packed to go, he launched one last, especially smooth projectile across the water, thinking this time, at last, he might reach the far bank. As it left his hand, he knew at once that it wasn't good enough. With an ineluctable sadness nesting in his heart, he turned away from his final pebble's too-high trajectory, not bothering to wait for the splash that would ordinarily give him such satisfaction.

'DONG-NG-NG-ng-ng . . .'

Rather than the predicted gulp of water, a clang of metal returned to him, a sound loud enough to set three . . . four . . . five echoes off into the hills, like a tolling bell or the sound of voices echoey in a dark tunnel.[17] Holding his breath, afraid that the rumours of terrible events were about to be proven true, Stefan turned. The steam disappeared from his face.

'*Was ist das?*' he asked himself, dismissing the idea that his stone might have struck a submerged log.

[My father held his breath too, widening his eyes in fearful anticipation. The first time he did this I quietly asked him to stop.]

Slowly, with a rumbling that echoed around the mountains like a storm, a thin arm — or was it a branch? — rose from the lake like a woman offering a sword to the air, or a harpoon stuck in the side of a giant whale, or . . . Before Stefan could add another simile, the huge spear was dwarfed by a turret, a tower of metal that shed the

17. This echo reminds me of the end of Carol Reed's film of *The Third Man*, when the authorities are pursuing Harry Lime through the sewers of Vienna. My favourite moment is the agonizingly slow walk of the heroine, Alida Valli, past Joseph Cotten waiting by his car in the cemetery's long avenue, but I also love the image of Lime's fingers poking through the holes of an immovable grille, like the first shoots of a plant reaching towards the sky, his escape blocked.

A few years ago, I met the son of Oswald Hafenrichter, the movie's Austrian editor. His father had told him that, while the footage of the streets was shot in post-war Vienna, the sewers through which Lime fled were actually beneath the City in London, the roaring water he splashes in, the submerged River Fleet. So, by the magic of editing, Orson Welles was in two countries at once, the air of Austria and the vaults of England.

lake's water by the gallon, a thundering waterfall that could have passed for a tourist attraction if such a thing had existed in that remote region of Austria. Stefan opened his mouth. His gasp was cloaked in steam. Slowly, the *Sousaphone* – though he didn't yet know its name – awoke from the depths of the lake, clanking, groaning irritably for having been disturbed, an unbelievable sight for a boy of thirteen.

'*Mein Gott*,' Stefan whispered, knowing no adult was present to hear him take the Lord's name in vain.

Not thinking that his life might be about to end, Stefan pulled the rucksack off his back, took out his sketchbook and began to draw the metallic monster two cricket pitches away from him. A brave boy, he sat on the bank, obscured, he believed, by the reeds. He stared at the black machine bobbing in the water.

'*Unglaublich*,' he murmured, shaking his head, his pencil moving quickly back and forth across the rough paper, outlining what he now realized was the hull of a vessel the likes of which he had never seen before. '*Unglaublich*.'

'DING-NG-NG-ng-ng . . .'

Just as he was colouring in the body of the craft, working to capture the shine of sky and water, a clang of metal on metal made him raise his head, and, as he held his breath again, a head gradually emerged from the turret halfway along the vessel. Then, he could just make out, hands raised a pair of binoculars.

'They must have heard the stone,' Stefan thought, dropping his sketchbook and lying flat on the damp grass. From the new angle on his back, he could see the full moon in the fathomless blue of the sky. The sun had slipped behind the mountains; it was evening, and he was a mile from the village without a light to guide him home. He thought of his parents, imagining their anger curdling into worry, and hoped they could forgive him what he was about to do.

'Hallo! HALLO!'

Before he quite knew what he was doing, Stefan was on his feet, wildly waving his arms, jumping up and down on the soggy grass, his toes as cold and wet as they would ever be, squelching, colder than they would be in all the adventures ahead of him.

From nowhere, it seemed, a powerful beam found him in the twilight dancing up and down. It buttered his face with light. Dazzled, he stopped his frantic waving to shield his eyes and listened to the sound of an engine — *chunka chunka chunka chunka* — growing louder and louder, the ripples that washed towards him growing bigger and bigger until they lapped his already frozen ankles. He must have been standing for a full ten minutes without moving a muscle, trying his best to see beyond the beam of golden light which grew brighter by the second until he was sure he could feel its heat.

'*Guten Abend*,' a deep voice rumbled high above him, like God, when the submarine had finally come to rest in

145

front of Stefan, plunging the little boy in its shadow. '*Wie gehts?*'

'*Gut, danke,*' Stefan replied, as if he talked to the owners of submarines every day of the week.

The dazzling beam was switched off, and, after a minute's worth of orange stars, Stefan adjusted his eyes to the gloom, by which time Kapitan Dunkel had fully emerged from his vessel and jumped ashore, landing beside Stefan with an almighty splosh. His cable-knit sweater glowed in the moonlight like the moon.

Stefan reassured Dunkel that he wasn't a master-spy working for a foreign power and was then invited on board for a tour. He wasn't entirely sure if Dunkel's suspicion was a joke because he took a prolonged interest in Stefan's sketchpad and pencils even as he was smiling; for which he used a little mouth engulfed by a spade-shaped beard.

Stefan was so excited he forgot what time it was. The misted gauges, shiny valves and pipes along the narrow corridors were captivating, the sudden bursts of steam like genies released from their bottles. He looked down, between the slats of the duckboard, into darkness.

'Does she leak?' Stefan asked Kapitan Dunkel, who laughed to himself as if laughter were a secret.

'*Nein, nein, nein,*' he whispered [one of my father's jokes]. 'She never leaks. Would you like me to show you?'

Stefan knew at once that this was an invitation to go for an underwater trip and, for the second time that evening, he pictured his parents waiting at home. This time, keen to go on an aquatic voyage, he was unable to decide whether to make their faces angry or concerned. Both moods resulted in punishment, though Stefan had to admit that his parents weren't the strictest in the village by a long chalk. Perhaps, he concluded, they hadn't even noticed his lateness.

'I should be going home,' Stefan replied. 'It's past my bedtime.'

Stefan could hear his own voice saying this and it didn't convince him. He recalled his father's advice about not talking to strangers but reasoned that, as these adults were wearing the uniform of the Austrian Navy, this must be an exception to the rule. (He had heard about exceptions to rules but this was the first time he'd tried one out. He liked it.)

'Perhaps for seven minutes,' Stefan said.

He hadn't noticed the extra steam billowing from the valves, nor the rumble of the engine growing to a metallic heartbeat in his ear, so busy had he been discussing the matter with his conscience. Dunkel didn't even turn around.

If Stefan had ever been in a lift he might have recognized the sudden lurch in his stomach.

Chunka chunka chunka chunka.

He liked the tune this submarine was making, its anthem of escape, the music of freedom, and imagined tons of water sleeving the vessel, clothing it with invisibility as it slipped from the world of air for what he knew, in his heart of hearts, was to be for longer than seven minutes.

It was Mrs Green who discovered Stefan's sodden drawings at the edge of the Turnersee[18] the following afternoon, when the village's entire adult population was out scouring the countryside for Stefan.

In spite of the runniness of the sketches, she recognized at once that the book belonged to Stefan. She had known all along that, as young as he was, the boy had a soft spot for her, and here was the evidence, her name drawn inside a heart on the cover of the pad.

18. Driving from Maria Wörth *en route* to the more sheltered Turnersee, 'You haven't got your belt on, Schultzy,' my father announced, then, turning to me, 'Book her, Dano.'

'Go back to sleep, you silly bugger,' my mother barked, as she fought with the belt, taking her hands off the wheel.

'Book her, Dano,' he repeated, and then, 'Oh no no no no no no no . . .' his voice dwindling like an echo.

Parking on a hill outside the dilapidated summer cottage of a friend of my mother's, we walked to the lake like a proper family, maintaining an awkward proximity. Although we hadn't travelled far, the air was still, the sun behind clouds that were thinning, becoming transparent, milky. The slope down to the water was steep enough to propel my father forward, so, for once, he was able to keep up with us.

'You won't get Charlie Farnsbarns to wet his tootsies,' he crowed.

MRS GREEN

Although it was a secluded lake with no town sprouting on its banks, a place too small for the guidebooks, we saw – as we reached the five-bar gate and the wooden toll-booth blocking our path – chalets, trees to shelter from the sun, manicured grass for pitching tents, and, by the waterside, a row of small shops selling ice-creams and plastic holiday-junk.

'Just keep walking,' my mother murmured ventriloquially.

Feigning an inability to speak German, ignoring the bilingual notice on the gate listing times and admission charges, my mother strode past the blond boy on duty.

'Helma!' my father groaned. 'What the hell are you doing?'

For a moment it seemed we might get away with it; then, in clear German, the boy called to my mother, whose position at the head of the party marked her out as our ringleader. She looked blankly at him and continued walking.

'You must pay to swim,' the boy said in perfect English.

'We know some people at the camp-site,' my mother replied, switching smoothly to Plan B.

Taking his register from behind the counter, 'At which position are they?' the friendly ginger-skinned attendant asked.

'Just pay the boy, Helma,' my father said.

'Down there,' my mother answered without blinking.

I looked down at my feet, then examined my bathing towel as if I might find salvation in its orange swirly pattern. My ears were on fire. Before anything else was said, my father fished

Before she knew what was happening, the sob in her throat turned to a full-blooded cry, alerting the gaggle of villagers thrashing the vegetation with sticks a few yards away of her awful discovery.

'*Hilfe! HILFE!*' she shouted, and a terrible echo resounded through the valley, finding its way to Stefan's

---

in his pocket for change, and, at the sound of the jingling, my mother began to sulk. Nothing serious – a downturn of the mouth, a quiet tutting – enough to show her disapproval of my father's capitulation, appalled by the cost of Austria. The attendant thanked us matter-of-factly, as if the incident was a regular occurrence, then we continued towards the water in silence.

'You can't take her anywhere,' my father said. 'Typical Austrian.'

'Don't start,' I snapped, agreeing with him but preferring silence.

'You're two of a kind,' he continued, transferring the attack as fluently as my mother had tried to con the attendant. 'Just like your mother.'

Then, to wind me up, he produced one of his bone-dry laughs, a Santa Claus *ho ho ho* crossed with an actor's breathing exercise, produced at the back of the throat. When I was a teenager, I used to imitate the laugh, a mirthless echo, though it didn't stop me feeling he had won. A little smile flickered across his face.

Although it was late afternoon on a day of changeable weather, there were a couple of dozen people sunbathing or splashing in the water. Reaching the water's edge, we settled under an immaculately topiaried tree, spreading our towels as

distraught parents at home, huddled in blankets beside a fire lit to assuage their shock.

No one could imagine, in the grief-stricken days that ensued, how Stefan had left them, slipping away from his old life in a submarine that followed an underground river unknown to the villagers, out of the lake and down to the

---

far away as we could from the large-bodied women, skinny girls and the handful of hairy-chested men. There were young couples and families with small children, the children splashing one another or launching themselves from a jetty while their parents watched. The oldest couple present, my mother and father began to strip down to the bathing costumes we'd agreed to wear that morning, my father wobbling on one leg as he took his trousers off.

'Aren't you getting changed?' my father asked, the struggle with his trousers causing him to breathe more noticeably.

I was sitting cross-legged on the orange towel, too hot in my long-sleeved shirt and jeans, sweat prickling my top lip, moistening my hairline.

'I don't think so.'

'Don't let your dingle-dongle dangle in the dust!'

'We came down for a swim,' my mother added mournfully.

A man bounded towards the jetty, his stomach juddering, then, arms wide, he belly-flopped on to the lake, throwing out a large sheet of water that scattered onlookers.

'Someone's got to mind the clothes.'

'Suit yourself,' my father said.

They turned and walked across the grass to the lake, my father, whiter than anyone else, looking down for anything sharp hidden in the grass, the bruise between his thumb and

sea ten miles away, occasionally scraping the cavern walls, the piercing wail of the hull identical to the noise Stefan's mother emitted when she heard the news that her son's sketchbook had been discovered abandoned beside the lake, the lake she would visit daily for the rest of her life.

---

forefinger still vivid. He tiptoed in, frail and skinny-legged alongside my mother, who strode onward, formidable as ever. Without pausing to test the temperature (this was, after all, a woman who refused injections at the dentist), she walked in as far as her waist then slid forward and under, holding her chin exaggeratedly high above the water, protecting everything from the jaw up as though water might spoil it for ever. Lagging behind, standing with the lake halfway between his knees and waist, scooping up handfuls of water to rub on his torso and arms to prepare for the shock of the cold, my father looked flimsy. The low-cholesterol diet he had started earlier that year had stripped him of pounds, but it didn't suit him.

He might have called 'Slow down, Helma,' but I couldn't be sure. He was already too far away.

The baptism over, he joined his wife with scarcely a splash, and, from where I sat, it could have been their courtship all over again, before the mistakes, all the years of regret still in front of them. They moved into deeper water, up to their necks in it, the V of their wake moving gently behind and away from them, dissipating like creases on an ironing-board, two heads vanishing behind a clump of rushes while I watched, trying to appear nonchalant among the sunbathers strewn on the grass. I stretched out under the tree, entirely in the shade, a passable imitation of myself at sixteen, an undertow of adolescent

Although a bright boy, Stefan was too young and curious to imagine the traumatic events unfolding in his wake. If he had, he would have demanded the Kapitan turn the submarine around at once and take him home.

'Where are we now?' he asked on the second day of

---

moodiness lapping my feet, dragging me under as I shut my eyes. I was back visiting my own childhood, where the growth of my hands and ears was always under scrutiny.

'He should be a pianist/surgeon/harpist/masseur...' a friend of the family murmurs.

'What size shoes/shirt/trousers does he take?' someone two foot shorter than me is asking, though nothing they give me requires a knowledge of my measurements.

My mother's tone of voice saying, 'Hasn't he grown taller?'

The screams of children thin to a squeak, lodging somewhere in my head where it can't trouble me, a squeak that metamorphoses into Kundl's duster removing the stubborn stains from Günther's planet. She moves like a Dalek from room to room until she reaches my bed. Invisible, I am watching her polish the mirror, the elephant, the blinds, the stool and the pillowcases, finishing on her hands and knees to search beneath the bed, where I've hidden my laden, incriminating suitcase, a case she reaches into the dark to retrieve...

'You should have come in,' my silhouetted father said breathlessly, replacing his spectacles, the lenses, like the perfect droplets on his body, catching the last of the sun.

A towel knotted around his waist, he was facing the lake where, reluctant as a child, my mother was only then emerging from the deep. Children stared.

'It was lovely,' he said. 'Not cold.'

his adventure, already ensconced in his own cabin and with the first of a series of sketches of life aboard a submarine attached to the hull.

'Sweden,' Kapitan Dunkel murmured without taking

The sun, in the course of its struggle to emerge from behind the clouds, had moved around, leaving me even more conspicuous. Fully clothed, no longer in the shade, I might have been an office worker sprawled in a park in the lunch hour, a refugee from his own life.

'You should have said something if you knew you weren't going to swim,' my mother muttered as we made our way back up the hill to the car. 'We paid to swim.'

I knew what was coming next and was wondering how best to cope as we reached the gate, the little hut and the metal cash-box hoarding our money. My mother approached the teenager behind the counter to begin what I knew was, despite the rapidity of her German, a protest that her son with the big hands had not gone in for a swim and could we have that portion of our entrance fee returned, *vielen danke*. She gestured grandly at me, insisting that, *schau*, her son wasn't in the least bit wet and obviously hadn't put either of his strikingly large feet into the lake, oh no.

'How many years have I put up with this?' my father said, as much to himself as anyone, and then he was off, puffing up the hill, heading for the car as though nothing was happening.

'Nearly fifty,' I said, running to catch up with him.

We drove back to Hari's through the dusk. My mother, who had failed to recoup a single groschen from the lake attendant, muttered about the manner in which her country had priced itself out of the tourist trade. Then she turned round to me to ask, 'Are you going to the toilet properly?'

his face from the eyepiece of the periscope Stefan was dying to use.

It was too soon to ask, he thought, and was wondering when would be the right time when the Kapitan turned to him and gestured with his hand.

When we finally arrived at Hari's bungalow, my father began turning out his pockets on the ledge beside the front door, talking to himself, mumbling 'Jesus . . . Jesus.' Light was spilling from porthole windows high on the wall on either side of the front door, so we knew my uncle was back from his trip to the war-zone.

'Ah, Jesus . . .' he said, 'I told you not to give me the key . . . Jesus Christ.'

A crumpled paper handkerchief, a credit-card receipt, a boiled sweet, a set of car keys. Laid on the wall, one by one, they were little more than shapes in the dusk to my father's eyes, the blue of the sky thickening, the suggestion of porch lights in the distance, crickets in the long grass on the far side of the road. He fumbled like a blinded man.

'Old fool!' my mother hissed, then, refusing to drop the matter even after she'd rung the bell, 'You tell Hari you lost it. I'm not.'

'*WER IST DAS?*' Harald, the older of my cousin Lianne's two children, bellowed from the other side of the door.

'*Tante Heli*,' my mother replied.

When Harald asked why she hadn't used her key, my mother commanded him to open up, which he did after rattling the lock theatrically. Fattened like Hansel, a boy about three feet tall opened the door, unflustered by the agitated adults in front of him. Showing no particular curiosity at the sight of the stranger with the big hands and feet who should have been a

'Thank you,' said Stefan, stepping forward, unwilling to show his excitement to the men he already considered his crewmates. 'Do I have to take an oath of secrecy?'

The world he saw was captivating. Caught in the submarine's dazzling beam of light, a cabaret of marine-life

---

surgeon, he stepped back to let us in then moved to the far corner of the living room to continue playing with his Gameboy, his endomorphic fingers stabbing the buttons. We were supposed to have returned earlier to see my cousin, who had driven from Weitra in the north to collect her sons after their trip south, but, while her eldest child was still up at half past ten, Lianne and her youngest boy had gone to bed.

'Shall we wake her up?' my mother asked, forgetting her irritation with my father. 'She'll be leaving early tomorrow, so you won't see her if you don't see her now. Perhaps I could fetch you at seven tomorrow morning, before she leaves. I said we should have gone to the cemetery before Hari got back.'

Lianne disliked returning home after her mother's death, where there were too many reminders of her bereavement, and, worse, evidence of Gerda above the sink in the bathroom and beside her father's bed.

His inhaler in his hand, my father slunk off while Harald dug out a torch and searched the car for the missing key, anything to delay bedtime.

'Servus, STEFAN!'

Hari emerged from his bedroom like Günther earlier in the week, dressed only in a pair of snow-white Y-fronts, his pendulous balls like a couple of apples. Gripping my hand firmly, he stepped back to appraise me as though I were a painting.

'You are tall now,' he said. 'Zooper!'

Before anything was said, my mother agitatedly explained

shimmied before the vessel, choreographed shoals dancing to the music of the engine, an octopus waving its empty hands like a conjurer, fish turning acrobatically in the black water while a shark loomed, ready to bring the curtain down on their act.

'*Sehr schön*,' Stefan breathed without taking his eyes from the spectacle, already planning his next drawing.

The Kapitan nodded sagely, grateful that the kidnapping of Stefan had gone smoother than he could have

---

to her younger brother about the missing key as he shrugged, speaking softly to his sister. I might have described his calmness as untypical of my Austrian family if I hadn't afterwards learnt that he had, during the process of pacifying her, complained in a reasonable voice that not only did he need to inform the police but that every lock would have to be changed at no small expense.

'Tomorrow,' he boomed, 'we EAT!' then disappeared into the kitchen.

My wheezing father sat on the edge of the bed in the guest room, pulling on his inhaler, trembling slightly as he did.

'She shouldn't have given it to me,' he said when he saw me in the doorway. 'Silly woman. I told her.'

My mother returned after a few minutes and was surprisingly restrained. The mattress sinking under her weight, she assured my father that Hari would return to the places we had visited that day to ask after the key.

'I'll take Stefan to Günther's.'

Her voice unnaturally quiet; the music of the Gameboy trilling in the next room; the terrible noise of my father's breathing.

hoped, relieved he didn't need to restrain a kicking and screaming boy in his brand new submarine, a Top Secret no one, not even a young boy, could be allowed to reveal to the rest of the world.

In the years that followed, Stefan grew to manhood at sea and among the denizens of its exotic ports, docking in bustling harbours around the world when shore-leave was due. Stefan and his shipmates explored the markets and kasbahs, transfixed by snakes emerging from wicker pots to a tune that reminded them of home, tempted by rugs perfect for their cramped cabins (if only rugs were allowed at sea), led down narrow alleyways by the aromas of delicious food, seduced into buying postcards they couldn't send.

The crew took to their unexpected guest, at first welcoming Stefan as a mascot for their perilous enterprise (no one talked about the dangers involved in being a submariner). Later, when they tackled their many missions with bravery and an aplomb befitting the cream of the Austrian Navy, they prized him as an invaluable member of the team, and no one retired from the submarine without first having an affectionate portrait executed by Stefan, the self-taught artist, a drawing they treasured to the ends of their days.

[Each time my father told the tale of Stefan the cabin-boy, a different adventure was involved: the submarine sailing upside down for miles on end without anyone aboard noticing, until keen-eyed Stefan looked through the periscope and explained why everyone's temples ached from the blood having rushed to their heads; the submarine angering a whale of Moby Dick proportions off the coast of Newfoundland, the beast pursuing the vessel down the coast of North America until, with a flick of its tail, it launched the craft on to dry land, where it crashed to earth in the branches of a tree on the East Coast; the whirlpool that sent it spinning anti-clockwise to the centre of the earth; the war with Hungary.

I scarcely remember the details of these stories now, there were generally so few; the crackle of the branches when the submarine crashed on to the tree, perhaps, or the whale's jaws as wide as a tunnel. The adventures were never the point for my father, who preferred luxuriating in the deep, among the dancing fish, by the caverns where the coiled eels lurked, lit by the light that struck the surface of the sea to pierce it like a miracle, the currents of the Seven Seas sending me to sleep.

The end of this tale was always the same, a melancholy slide into silence my father must have hoped I would never hear, the moment when the jolly dad I knew turned slowly into the introspective creature never encountered by day, as if metamorphosing into my melancholy mother as I drifted off. His stories were, after all, more dream than reality by the time they were over.]

Stefan returned home in the 1960s, long after the Second

World War, an old man. To look at him — as the little children playing with a hula hoop in the street did when he passed by — you would never have suspected he had travelled seventeen times around the world in the battered *Sousaphone* and its replacement *Sousaphone II*; and most of those miles underwater. He was a real adventurer, slipping through the streets of a village changed beyond recognition: fresh houses where fields had been; supermarkets where there used to be family businesses whose owners once knew Stefan's birthday and celebrated it with sweets; the surnames on doorbells a sure sign the world had moved on without him, changed for ever. The names were unfamiliar, though didn't a Haubmann once tease him in the playground for having a bald father? And wasn't the blonde girl with pigtails he sat next to in class called Hausberger? He couldn't remember. Even memories of his mother and father had faded.

So he walked to the outskirts of the village, slowly along the road where once he had sprinted to escape the adults who patted his head as if he were a dog. He climbed the hill (puffing, puffing hard) to visit one last time the lake where the adventures of a lifetime had started, the place where his parents had erected a plaque to look out across the lake [were there really so many memorials in my father's tales?]. The legacy of a grieving village, it was barely legible after fifty years of weather, but Stefan's beautifully carved name was holding on, above an inscription chosen by his parents:

He loved light, freedom, and animals.[19]

He selects a stone, the smoothest he can find in the long grass, and, despite the arthritis turning him to marble, launches it out, over the lake, towards the mountains that haven't changed one bit since he last stood there, a little boy, hoping to reach the other side.

Is there a splash? Or does he, at last, achieve the one ambition left to him, to find the far bank at last?

If my father were here I would ask him.

19. An inscription on the grave of one of the children who died in the Aberfan disaster, 21 October 1966.

6.

GAMMON

A little-remembered vogue for potholing developed among the bored nobility of the Austro-Hungarian Empire in the late nineteenth century. Foremost among its exponents was Thomas von Gammon, so avid an explorer of underground caves and tunnels that his long-suffering wife often failed to recognize him on his return from lengthier expeditions, his face pallid after months below ground, his straggly beard hiding his tell-tale duelling scar, fungal growth on his clothes and skin, the pads of his fingertips so rough that the family hounds would growl if he petted them. His children saw him as an unseasonal, nightmarish Father Christmas, his sacks of foul-smelling objects from the centre of the earth a nasty parody of the munificence of Santa Claus.

Entering the grand reception area of his dazzling mansion unrecognized by the servants who, nevertheless, could identify good breeding no matter what the smell, no matter how poor the rags, 'I'm home,' he would whisper, unused to the sound of his own voice.

'Who are you?' his youngest daughter asked him once, confronted by a strange creature dripping viscous lime-green and crimson goo on the marble chessboard floor.

'Your father,' her father replied.

'We don't have a father,' she replied, and her father decided there and then that his days of potholing would have to come to an end, that he should settle down to a peaceful retirement in Obdach, his furthest journey to and from the monastery at Seckau.[20]

However, there was one last district of caverns near the border with France that Thomas von Gammon hoped to investigate before he hung up his candles, his ropes, and his clumpy boots. He had heard talk of them one evening in a tavern somewhere in Peru, during the years of his search for the legendary caverns of the Incas, reputed to be large enough to mount state banquets in: servants,

---

20. When, after twenty years, I finally visited the area of Gammon's dream-retirement, I wondered, as we drove through the pristine countryside, if he could have stomached the quiet life.

Never allowed to visit Obdach as a child, I was left to play Monopoly with my cousin (though buying and selling the streets of Vienna never seemed right) while the adults trooped off to the festival that was held one Sunday in August, returning hours later, swaying, their unintelligible voices slurred, their breath smelly, too kissy-kissy for my liking. Any town that could so transform people must be an awful one, I reasoned.

That year, the festival fell on the day before my flight home, my last chance to be alone in my Uncle Günther's house. I had gone to bed the previous evening, after Hari's guest-house treat, woozy from the large glasses of watered-down wine.

I was unused to alcohol, having taken my mother's adventures as a salutary reminder of how wrong things could go,

chefs, food-tasters and pets all on one long table without anyone having to budge up. Nobody ever questioned Thomas on the point of locating a cavern capable of holding such banquets. It was left unspoken that the need to discover was everything. If the object of the quest had some use, however bizarre, all the better. First and foremost, Thomas was, like all explorers, an artist of the unknown world, for whom geography was the palette on which he mixed his adventures.

'There is a series of caves in the heart of Europe,' his Peruvian drinking-companion murmured one cool evening, 'said to include a network of natural canals which connect all the countries of the continent. Señor, to find

---

though hers wasn't the only lesson I had needed. Blue-faced and breathless, I was rushed to hospital during my first week-end at university, comatose from the fifty sherries I had downed over a ninety-minute period, a foolish record I was egged on to break.

Günther's house was still, the only sound the familiar noises of work from the other side of the road, the shuddery clang and clunk of metal poles and planks, the thud of something large reaching the end of a chute then fragmenting, the cement mixer chugging in the background. My uncle had left the house noiselessly, to prepare for the lunch he had promised us, though I felt sure he was expecting Kundl to provide ingredients and most of the labour. Before I could take the opportunity to unload my suitcase of the treasured bits and pieces I had brought with me, I heard the front door open and, tiptoeing to the window, balancing my head on my shoulders, tried not to

these caves would be the crowning achievement of your career as the bravest adventurer of his day, if not of all time. A name to set beside Raleigh and Cortez.'

Wary of flattery and suspecting his companion was distracting him from the task at hand – acquiring for the Austro-Hungarian Empire the largest single cave in the known world – von Gammon paid little attention to the words of his guide.

Yet this fabled place continued to haunt his subconscious for many years and, on the afternoon his daughter

---

spill my brains. My parents' car was parked in front of the gate.

'Get out of that pit, laddie!'

On the other side of my bedroom door, my father was taking the opportunity to use Günther's smelly bathroom – his pee, aimed expertly to avoid the shelf, thundering in the bowl – while, downstairs, my mother ransacked her brother's cupboards for morsels, a twenty-one-gun salute of kitchen-cabinet doors. That done, the pair of them took it in turns to lecture me.

'You should have been dressed hours ago . . .'

'This is the best part of the day . . .

'We've been up for hours . . .'

After '. . . I said we'd be at Christl's by nine . . .' my mother burst into the room without so much as a knock and despite my protestations that I was thirty-one, for heaven's sake.

'There's nothing I haven't seen before,' she countered, when I protested. I was too sleepy to argue.

Swinging hypnotically from the rear-view mirror, a cardboard fir tree embalmed the car with a dizzying smell of pine. We arrived at Christl's five minutes early, my mother going to

looked perplexed at the sight of her own father squelching through the palatial home, the thought of this mythical place bubbled to the surface once again.

'Think of it, my darling,' he said that evening to his wife who, up till then, had believed she had her husband home for good. 'A fitting way to crown my years of exploration. A discovery at the very heart of Europe, a legacy for our children and our children's children.'

His wife, who had long since forgotten how to hold a conversation with her smelly husband, sighed and shook

---

call for my aunt and Ernst while my father and I sat on a bench outside the building like a couple of old friends, our heads tipped back to catch the morning sun, welcome after the previous day's rain. Our faces glowed, our skins beginning to warm.

'Not bad, eh, wuss?'

When they emerged ten minutes later, Ernst – his hair sticking up, his shirt sticking out – confessed with a broad grin that he'd only got out of bed ten minutes earlier, *ja, wirklich*. Impossible to read, Christl was wearing a pair of Mafioso sunglasses.

'*Grüss Gott! Grüss Gott!*'

Following her dusty car through the vacant countryside to Obdach, we entered the town via a diversion that led to a makeshift car park at the back of the town centre. The centre was a single thoroughfare with a baker's and a few clothes shops that hadn't changed their windows for a decade, one displaying wedding dresses, explosions of lace, voluminous sleeves and endless, dragging trains.

her head, taking care not to breathe in too deeply before replying.

'You musd do as you see fid,' she said nasally, 'but dever delude yourselve that wad you do is for the benefid of the children, dor even the Emperor. A dobleman's god to do what a dobleman's god to do. And you explore.'

[My father was never very good at dialogue, and, even

At the *Fest*, guest-houses and cafés set tables and stalls along the main street for visitors and locals to drink and eat all day and into the evening to the accompaniment of yodellers and oompah bands until, yodelling themselves, they sank into a convivial stupor.

We were early and it was still quiet. People were creating their stalls, unfolding trellis tables and covering them with cloths, erecting A-frames with handwritten posters, setting out napkins, plates and Tupperware containers of food, and lighting barbecues, while musicians, with trombone, clarinet and accordion at the ready, tested microphones.

'*Ein, zwei . . . ein, zwei . . .*'

Impatient, the early risers paced the street like boxers, fifteen gruelling rounds of food, drink and relentlessly upbeat music in front of them. My mother, tormented by the smells, knew there would be trouble if our appetites were ruined before Günther's mushroom goulash. Although it was only a little past eleven in the morning, the sun was hot in the empty sky so we decided on a drink. While my mother and Christl looked for a table they could agree on, my father and Ernst stood together, Dad nodding and smiling vigorously, Ernst stepping from foot to foot.

'Ernst,' my father said, '*schön*.'

at the age of six, I could spot his borrowings from Hollywood or pulp fiction.]

'I am only grateful that you support me in this venture,' her obtuse husband replied, beginning to make plans for the expedition even before dessert was set before the couple by servants with pegs on their noses.

Thomas von Gammon was to see in the new century

'*Ja*,' said Ernst. '*Schön.*'

The five of us squeezed around a picnic table then began to fiddle with the sun-umbrella while a three-piece yodelling combo in *lederhosen* began to punish the silence, *ree-d'Ee-dee-o* . . .

'Remember this?' my father asked me, then, before I could answer, turned to Christl and Ernst, continuing, 'Helma . . . listened . . .' then, turning to my mother, 'What's "listened" in German?' – she flapped him away without supplying a translation – 'Helma . . . listened . . . to THIS' (pointing to the stage) 'for *zwei Jahr*, every *Tag*.'

'*Jahren*,' my mother added.

Christl and Ernst smiled, nodded, emitted an 'Ah' of comprehension.

After photographs – Ernst holding a glass of beer aloft, my grinning father doing likewise, my mother glum behind her watery, Spritzer smile (she was driving) – I strolled back up the street.

The place was coming to life. Leaving the pained yodellers behind, past the wedding dresses, I stopped opposite the second stage, the one my mother had decided not to sit near because she suspected the music would be less traditional. The band went at it with gusto, rocking from side to side,

underground, singing to himself by the light of two candles somewhere beneath the border of Germany and France. Staying in the bowels of the earth for months with only a team of mules for company, von Gammon followed dead end after dead end. His frequent exhalations of disappointment in the face of a tremulous candle would

---

nursing their accordions as though they were beloved heirs, tapping their feet in time, producing a sound almost identical to the row at the far end of the street, where, even then, my mother was being transported back to the days of her worst depressions. 'A miserable bugger,' as my father would say. I could only assume she thought this crew would turn out to be anarchic because several band-members were under forty.

The street was beginning to fill with women in dirndls and white blouses, and, shoulder to shoulder, men in the *Steirer Anzug*, the grey and dark-green velvety local outfits, uniforms to differentiate one region from another. They floated, impeccably groomed, round the litterless town. Smiling at one another, greeting friends with their arms open wide, they raised glasses without the pretext of a camera to capture the moment, over-acting like extras in a lost Leni Riefenstahl documentary. Dancing began in the spaces between stalls, feathers in hats bobbing above the crowds, a windswept cornfield, the crowd parting for the couples who, like toy cars, changed direction the moment they bumped someone.

'Ah, Stefan,' Christl said as I returned to the table. 'Later. After you have been to your uncle's. We go to Seckau. Yes?'

When he wasn't sweating over the spits, one of the chefs hurtled up and down the street on a child's scooter, blowing a referee's whistle, with a home-made advertisement for the

leave him in a Stygian gloom it took minutes of fumbling among his equipment for a match to dispel.

'There is no such place,' he said one day or night (he didn't know), and wondered how long he had been talking to himself.

'It's the first sign of madness,' he said.

---

chickens pinned to his back. Revellers cleared a path for him. Unable to resist the hard sell, Ernst and Christl were being served as I sat down.

'You remember the monastery,' my mother added.

Before I could say anything, Ernst, who knew the waitress, dropped his voice to ask for salt, discarding the role of Amiable Dolt he had played up till then. Christl seemed put out by his manner, though nothing was said, and when the woman had wiped her greasy palms on her apron and returned to her stall, the two of them tucked in as if nothing had happened.

'No,' I said, as a second member of the chicken-stall arrived with a plate which he set before my mother.

By now, she was affording my father more shade than the sun-umbrella.

'Don't say I didn't warn you,' my father sang as she tucked in.

Travelling up and down the street, the mock steam-engine pulling two wagons full of children rumbled passed. The driver waved at Ernst then turned to say something to the man beside him in the cab, who also waved, laughing extravagantly as he did. Ernst returned a diluted smile then licked his fingers. The engine tooted steam. Chugging up the sloping road, it was followed by a couple of boys squirting water pistols at a third boy in the back seat.

'Be quiet, Edward,' my mother replied, her cheeks bulging.

*

'What is?' he said.

'Talking to yourself,' he said.

'I'm fine ... fine ... fine ... fine ...'

The word bounced around the slimy corners of the

At the heart of the village of Seckau stands the eight-hundred-year-old monastery where we'd arranged to meet Christl and Ernst after what turned out to be a disastrous lunch at my Uncle Günther's. On the drive there, full to bursting, the seat-belt taut across her bosom, my mother had pointed out mountains she claimed her brother regularly ran up to keep fit, only to change her mind when another peak came into view. All the way, a little deaf, my father echoed her like a gully.

'That's one, isn't it, Fred?' my father trilled. '*Schön.*'

I was silent in the back seat, strapped in, trying to imagine what Günther might say to my mother when we returned that evening.

We disembarked in the shadowy, desolate streets. Looking tired as he struggled out of the passenger's seat, my father produced low, catarrhal coughs audible at the far end of the village, and when he breathed, his chest was full of kittens, kittens in a bag, ready for drowning.

'*Schwammerl,*' my mother enunciated. '*Schwammerl.*'

'And that's "mushrooms", is it?' my father replied.

Christl and Ernst pulled up as we were shuffling our feet outside the main gate, my father's German lesson postponed.

'Stefan,' Christl said in her halting English, touching the bonnet of a black car parked outside the monastery, 'this car ... belongs to an Englishman who has ... for five years, been in Austria.'

'Really,' I said, my mind at my uncle's, though I tried to look

174

cavern, mocking him in the manner that makes echoes especially bad company.

He lost track of the days he had been entombed, the number of passages he had followed, the number of walls

---

as interested as my mother, who immediately began to quiz Christl.

'I've seen all this before, missus.'

Still wheezy, my father rested on a bench near the gift shop and studied the still-dark skin between his thumb and fore-finger. The rest of us walked briskly around the church, posing for Ernst's camera beside the chapel where Christl's grand-children had been baptized. My face was made of stone. His film wound on another frame, Ernst beetled off to collar the Englishman, waist-deep in a class of Seckau's *Abteigymnasium* – shoulder-bags, braces, shorts and chatter – his curly blond hair receding, an ageing cherub adrift on a cloud of children.

He greeted us first in German and then – 'Gosh, we don't get many British here' – in rusty English that had come to sound, after years of exile, like a second language. His knees, exposed by a pair of khaki shorts, were pink and vulnerable. A soft-spoken, red-faced man in his forties, he behaved as though he had woken up in Paradise hardly able to believe his luck. Talking about his initial difficulties with the language in this part of Austria – how '*Ich weiße nicht*' becomes '*I'waß nett*' – he was relieved to have mastered the local shibboleths.

'Well, I can say it took some while.'

Christl laughed, flirtatiously I thought, at his analysis of the local dialect, and then, at Ernst the policeman's request, he gave us the tour, into a cellar where they made schnapps, huge metal vats of the stuff, and then on to the monastery garden, a great tract of land striped with vegetable plots and

he had come up against. His maps, recording the directions he had tried, began to resemble a plate of spaghetti. He was down to his last hundred candles.

'SHOW YOURSELF,' he boomed, frustrated and

---

thick with fruit trees, the whole lot tended by one woman in her eighties. 'An amazing lady.'

I caught him looking up to my mother, aghast at the size of this miracle of God's. She began to talk about her allotment back home but he was off before she got going, leading us down an avenue of fruit trees. Armfuls of bees hung heavily around us. Barely able to remain aloft, they collapsed into flowers as though glad to take the weight off their wings. Their chosen petals shuddered like diving boards in the still afternoon.

'Did you hear that?' my mother crooned. 'He said he would never go back to his garden centre in Chester.'

At the end of our tour, we were exhorted to visit the gift shop by the Englishman whose name we never learnt. Ernst slid a few notes into his hand, which he accepted without a flicker of his pale, angelic eyes, returning to his children with a spring in his step, the backs of his knees as pitiful as the knees themselves. I alone took his hint, entering the standard-issue shop: glass shelves, dolls packaged in plastic cubicles, novelty gonks for the ends of pencils.

'Nicht verstehen,' I muttered, 'nicht verstehen,' hoping that the monk plaguing me to buy an ugly, bone hair-slide couldn't speak English.

Catching my reflection in a mirror barnacled with seashells, I scarcely knew who I was, the effort I had made not to arouse my mother's suspicions warping my facial muscles. The gift shop had temporarily allowed me to relax into a shape that

close to tears, thumping the cavern wall till his fists were bleeding [thumping as hard as your mother bangs the slices of meat for our *Wiener Schnitzel*, my father added].

Startled, the mules reared up, and, with an ominous

---

better represented my feelings. Now I looked like my own passport photograph.

'You should have come with us,' my mother said to my father, still sitting on the bench where we'd left him, an hour earlier, with nothing to do but listen to his lungs and examine his bruise.

'How are you feeling, Edi?' Christl asked, bowing to talk to him.

'Not too bad, Christl,' he replied jollily. 'Not too bad.'

On the way out, we passed the gardener inching her way home after a day at work. With her walking-stick and her stoop, she looked like a child's impersonation of old age, or the letter n.

Ernst provided the rest of this tour of his home patch, continuing with the guest-house-cum-hotel next to the monastery. In what was becoming a characteristic use of his status in the community, he took a member of the hotel staff aside, and, within seconds of entering, we were poking our heads round the door of the dining hall, testing the sofas, nosing around the upstairs landing. The place had recently been redecorated like a 1980s branch of Next: pale floorboards; rugs; antique furniture; and large, healthy rubber-plants trailing along the floor. One ceiling appeared to be decorated with what looked like an original mural half rescued from layers of paint, or it might have been a clever reproduction half finished. Either way, my father – who had, by this time, rallied – took its photograph.

rumble, the walls on either side of him began to shake. Flakes of stone showered his helmet, playing him as though he were a xylophone, the mules braying and skittering like children in a Fun House, a strange tune emanating from his head.

From there we strolled to Ernst's office, empty on a Sunday and dingy for want of windows to admit the sunny afternoon. Wiped clean of dust and fingerprints, too immaculate for the scene of a crime, it appeared unused, the cellophane that had wrapped it just then thrown into the wastepaper basket. Obviously, there was nothing much to do here except exist. Apart from the occasional driving offence, the life of an officer of the Seckau gendarmerie must be a doddle.

Ernst took us proudly from room to room, like a child with his latest toy. Showing us his corner, he plonked himself in the leather chair at his desk, beaming, then took us into the boss's office to see the desk, the shiny name-plate, and the chair Ernst was probably hoping to occupy one day. He spun round in it.

'*Schau*,' he said, beaming at us a second time when he'd leapt from the seat with a farting noise.

A tiny motor buzzed and the blind rose up the window of the chief's office, letting in a few rays of light and a view of the brick wall of the building opposite.

'*Schön*,' my father murmured.

Ernst demonstrated the fridge, offering us a can of own-brand Coke from its disinfected shelves, then led us to the uniforms hanging from pegs on the wall beside a map of his department's jurisdiction. As we were leaving, my father tried on Ernst's white peaked cap then, holding my collar as though

'Plink . . . plonk plonk plonk . . . Plink . . . plonk.'

So intent was Thomas von Gammon on the shaking walls that he didn't notice the crack opening up in the ground beneath his feet, spreading inexorably like wrinkles, like a horrible grin, until, too late, he was hurtling

---

arresting me, posed for a photograph, staring pop-eyed at the camera, grinning. The light from the ceiling glinted on his spectacles. Christl laughed and, nodding in amusement, Ernst looked happy to be accepted.

'When people see that, they'll think you were drunk!' my mother boomed, then repeated it in German to Christl and Ernst, who laughed again.

Everyone laughed.

While my father and Ernst returned to the monastery for the cars, Christl, my mother and I ambled through the deserted streets and on to Ernst's house on the outskirts. We paused at a pink house opposite a shrine to Our Lady on an island in the middle of the road.

'This used to be Ernst's,' my mother piped, pleased to be in the know.

Looking uncomfortable, her lips thinned to a pencil line, a cancellation striking out her good mood, Christl explained through my mother that it now belonged to his ex-wife's nephew.

When Christl's Seat Ibiza and my parents' silver Toyota pulled up beside us, the brakes squeaking irritably, we drove the rest of the way to Ernst's house.

He had divided the place into two flats, him downstairs and an elderly couple renting the three rooms overhead. The communal hallway and stairs were neglected, the carpets

down the chasm that yawned beneath him, riding on the seat of his reinforced leather breeches, down into an even darker darkness.

'Aaaaaaah,' he cried, completely forgetting his breeding, 'aaaaaaaaaaaaaaaaaaaaaaaaah . . .'

Behind him he could hear the complaining mules on

———————

fraying at the edges like Dougal from *The Magic Roundabout*, dead plants on the sill, grimy windows, a pile of useless letters on an unloved, scruffy stool outside the door to Ernst's portion of the house. Assembled wonkily from individual letters, like a ransom note, his name was glued on the hardboard door. By the look and smell of the place – it appeared to have been shut up for the summer – no one was about to pay up to secure its freedom.

'Oh,' my mother murmured, not realizing she had made a sound.

It might have been a crime scene, or the home of an elderly man who, unseen for weeks, is rotting in an armchair.

His adult children's bits and pieces were everywhere: books and magazines, a suitcase, pots, pans, shoes, cushions from sofas stacked high on either side of the window (but no sign of the sofas). The furnishings were stale from neglect, the air seeded with the unmistakable perfume of a teenage boy, of a man without a woman. Dust on the fridge, unwashed trousers, shirts and socks, things left where they were last used, a pot of jam on the table, a pair of scissors on the portable TV, a coffee cup on the floor. A place unswabbed by cleaning fluids, it was impossible to imagine Christl sleeping there.

'I have not for many days been here,' Ernst said.

There was little boyishness left by the time he had drawn

their way after him, hoofs first, their long, prickly ears flapping behind them, their eyes showing the whites.

'Crushed to death by beasts!' he bellowed. 'This cannot be . . .'

His straggly beard blowing across his face, he seemed to fall for an eternity, leaving behind the moaning of his

---

the curtains to let in dusty light then tended to the answer machine's seventeen messages, which he listened to distractedly, opening windows as he did, stopping the tape in places to rewind it. Young voices, they must have been his children.

While Ernst continued to pick his way among the debris we moved into the garden to sit at a picnic table with a view of a mountain that my mother thought Günther might have sprinted up once upon a time.

'Well, what do you think of Seckau?' my father said. 'It's very peaceful, isn't it?'

'Of course it is,' my mother barked.

When Christl left the table to help Ernst with the drinks, my mother launched into a monologue in response to my question 'How long have they been together?'

'About six months: he had somebody else after his wife: he's got a seven-year-old son but he didn't marry the woman: she lives in Graz.'

She ran together disparate elements of people's lives in a stream-of-consciousness biography. Anything might have been connected to anything else. All details carried equal weight. The sun rises in the east because Ernst's ex-wife's nephew owns the pink house in Seckau.

After a few minutes, Ernst brought out seat-covers and drinks

team of mules as he continued to plummet, holding on to a pair of candles as though they were shrunken ski-poles, losing all sense of fear. His shoes had nearly worn away and his trousers were thinning to the denier of tissue paper. The fall was stripping away the layers of him, the

---

while Christl wiped crusty birdshit from the table-top with a wet rag. Suds oozed between her fingers, bubbling around the band of white skin her wedding ring had left. The wine glasses were different shapes, filmed with grease-fused dust, still wearing their Arcoroc labels. There were too few to go around, so Christl shared Ernst's.

'For how much longer are you here?' Christl asked when the shit had been erased and she'd joined us in a drink.

While I sipped beer from a tooth mug, 'He's leaving tomorrow,' my mother replied.

Playing the host, unable to sit still, Ernst rose, picked a fistful of puny, wild strawberries from his garden, then returned with them in a bowl, and, clamped in his armpit, three hefty photo albums large as LPs and fat as Bibles. One was devoted to his family, one to his early years as a police cadet and policeman, and one was of his father's seventieth-birthday holiday in Crete.

'*Schön*', my father called, raising his glass to signify that it was the wine he was praising.

The first padded album fell open with a thump. Minutes later, we were taken through the life of a man we had met for the first time three days earlier. He began with his father's holiday.

'*Und hier* he is. At the airport . . .' '*Und hier* on steps of the aeroplane . . .'

We nodded, passed the album respectfully around or craned

trappings that had made him who he was, the honours, the finery, the manners.

'This is it,' he said, deciding these would be his last words, though, with nobody there to record them, the gesture was futile.

---

to look, scarcely stretching the muscles of our necks to catch a page, there were so many to see. Bronzed and toned, Ernst and his dad looked like a vacationing gay couple. There were photographs of his robust father posing like Charles Atlas, tanning on the beach or raising a glass in the hotel lounge; so many photographs of individual moments – his arm halfway up, then aloft, then down to take a drink – that they could have been turned into animation, a flicker book. The pictures were mounted close together; the text, in spidery, gothic lettering beneath each one, was worthy of a museum curator: *Vati ins Wasser* or *Vati ins Hotel*.

In contrast, the album devoted to his family looked like the aftermath of a piece of Stalinist revisionism expunging the out-of-favour from the official version of history. It traced the end of Ernst's teenage years, through marriage and back to bachelorhood. Many of the pages given over to his married years displayed a single image surrounded by sticky hinges where others had been. The cellophane dividers in the album stuck to their pages. Ernst peeled them apart to reveal a single snapshot in a tundra of black card. Looking at him ageing, seeing his wife grow visibly tired, his children reach his chest, then his shoulders, then beyond – as though they were quick-sand and he was sinking into them – I wondered how much Ernst and his estranged wife had haggled over who took what. The afternoon at the lake for him, the day in Graz for her, the

[Something miraculous happened to Thomas at this juncture, but I can never remember what that was. While I recall my father's descriptions of the threadbare trousers, the battered shoes, and the fact that our hero was deeper

---

ownership of the children dribbling ice-cream down their chins settled by the toss of a coin.

In the last few pages, the photographs of Ernst on holiday turned Christl morose. Out of earshot of my mother and father, who were looking for places in Crete they might have recognized from their own photo album, she made a sarcastic comment about Ernst and his girlfriends, three or four in separate photographs, their arms hooked round his arm, his smile identical in every one. He became even more attentive then, kissing Christl on the cheek, draping his arm around her neck, filling her glass. I didn't need to speak German to recognize crawling, and I wasn't so surprised to hear, six months later, that they had parted company, and that my aunt was seeing a teacher.

For once, my parents were oblivious, trawling through the pictures of Crete, remembering a holiday they had taken when I was eighteen and sitting my university entrance exams. Sipping my wine, I thought it looked like rain.

'That's where we stayed.'

'Nah.'

'It *is*, Edward.'

'Suit yourself, Bertha.'

Like Otto von Otto, my father had finally caught his breath after the worst day of the holiday, and now he was on form, balancing the album like a hymn book, the cut on his hand still fierce although there was, at last, a streak of saffron, the first signs of skin healing. The promise of a sunrise.

underground than the Dan-yr-Ogof caves,[21] I have no idea how Thomas von Gammon survived his deadly plunge to the centre of the earth, nor how exactly he discovered the network of canals that, as the Peruvian guide had told him years earlier, linked the countries of Europe like veins.]

'At last,' he said, a ragged nobody at the centre of the earth. 'At last.'

It was a reverential whisper that might have suggested Thomas was confronted by a church, though what he raised his candle to consider was far from a holy place. It stank more vilely than he ever did, a green gelatinous substance running off the walls, the water blacker than any water he had ever seen, the colour of tar, of blood in a black-and-white film. As he raised his candle above his head, the high roof of the cavern glittered like stars, though the pervading smell of dampness and the eerie echo never allowed von Gammon to forget that he was entombed.

'At last!' he said again. 'My crowning glory.'

'Glory . . . ory . . . ory . . . ory . . .'

Able to walk gingerly along the slimy banks of this

21. A popular attraction in South Wales, fun for all the family in the 1960s and '70s, though I have no memory of going there. Nor, for that matter, do I remember our trip to Portmeirion, the Italianate village in North Wales where they filmed *The Prisoner*, surreal episodes from the captivity of a retired spy.

hellish waterway, he followed its course through tunnels stretching far beyond the meagre light of his candle, intestinal corridors that wound through rock for miles and miles, coiling around his dreams when he slept by the banks of his longed-for canal. And when he marched, shoals of eyeless fish followed him, their silvery bodies lit by the feeble flame of his candle.

After weeks of tedious journeying back the way he had come, somehow able to untangle the map, walking as if he were scenting the faintest trail of fresh air drifting from the meadows of the world above, his wife's perfume, the skin of his children washed and ready for bed, von Gammon returned to the light of a new century, a century of Progress, of Hope, of New Beginnings. The sunlight stung his eyes.

Underground for so long, he was forced to wear a blindfold for the first month of his return. This spared him the looks of horror on the faces of his wife and children, who had never seen him quite so ruined by his exploits: the scarring, the stench, the inhumanity of what stood before them that morning in March, led by a man-servant into the hall. A compost heap.

'My dear,' was all his wife could gasp, stifling a sob, too much of a lady to vomit.

Realizing her husband was temporarily blind, she allowed herself a grimace whenever the need arose, maintaining at all times the even tone of acceptance that was a true indication of her breeding.

Alas, his discovery was not greeted with the fanfares he had expected. The world was preoccupied with other matters when he emerged: the Boer War, influenza, the Boxer Rebellion, preparations for the World Exhibition in Paris. Thomas von Gammon spoke to newspapers, yes, though they relegated his claims to the inside pages, alongside reports of the latest hair tonics or cures for rheumatism, undignified company for such a hero, even if the nostrums on offer were wondrous indeed.

THE GENTLEMAN'S HAIR PREPARATION[22]

A Miracle in a Bottle for Only 2/-

Soon his extraordinary adventures were forgotten by a fickle public. A people priding themselves on their lack of gullibility, the Austrians had never entirely believed their countryman's fanciful tales of an underground world of intricate canals and blind fish in the first place, as much

22. How sorry for himself my father really felt about baldness, combing strands of hair across his scalp by the time he was forty-five, I couldn't say, though he never exhibited my mother's self-pity. In fact, he made light of his loss, marvelling at the quality of the wigs worn by Bing Crosby or Frank Sinatra, and promising himself a 'syrup' as soon as he won the football pools. Two memories. 1) Returning home from the Infants in tears convinced my daddy, older than the other children's parents, was going to die at any second. My mother comforted me while my father looked on, bemused. 2) The sight of Benny

as they had wanted to fall for the romance of the whole idea.

'There is a man outside to see you,' Mrs von Gammon announced to her husband one morning in 1915. 'He says he is from the War Ministry.'

Hill slapping the bald head of one of his comedy sidekicks. I couldn't see what was funny about it, and, stretched out on the rug in front of the television, cried about that as well.

So I was a sensitive, sentimental child, first frightened and then embarrassed by my father's impending senility, or mocked by my fellow pupils for having a mother and father so anatomically mismatched that everyone turned to look when they arrived at the school for Christmas concerts or parents' evenings. Teachers fiddled with their red biros or stared at the parquet. My mother's reputation as a tough cookie clung to her. Unbeknownst to me, I entered Portmead School trailing an air of menace.

By the time I left junior school, however, my mother was a different person. Even before the death of her parents she had become dissatisfied with her life, spending more evenings out, allowing me to see her drunk. This was a cause of puzzlement when I was eleven and disgust by the time puberty transformed me into a gangling, spotty misfit, locked in my room with Pink Floyd's *The Dark Side of the Moon*. So, all the changes came together: the deaths of my Austrian grandparents, our move to the coast, secondary school, and the ugly process of growing.

'We should have called you Dennis,' my father complained. 'Dennis the Menace.'

At the time, the prospect of a new home was worse than any

By now a broken man who greatly resented the outside world's indifference to his exploits, von Gammon looked at his wife with the dead eyes of disappointment, the loneliness of failure.

He was, by now, an alcoholic, and it showed in his

---

of the above, so I threw a tantrum worthy of an Austrian, an extravaganza of pouting, the kind my father had spent his married life escaping with photography and then model railways.

'Look how you've brought him up,' he moaned on the spring afternoon they announced our house was on the market. 'A spoilt brat!'

'I don't want to leave,' I bellowed. 'All my friends are here.' Then I pushed a fishfinger around my chip-greasy plate. 'You're not considering me!'

'Be quiet,' my mother growled, excavating a hillock of food, 'or you'll feel the back of my hand.'

I began mashing the fishfinger under my fork, torturing it, reducing it to an inedible, white and orange mulch.

'We can't leave now! What about my new school?'

'Now is the best time,' my mother added. 'Before you've settled in.'

Next door, the Beynons were shouting at the tops of their voices, first the squeal of Mrs Beynon, then her husband's thunderous bass, a pitched battle about a cat. I was going to miss this neighbourhood, I thought, momentarily aware of my own fit and how clinically I was directing it.

'I don't want to catch a bus every day!'

Their cutlery in their fists, poised at either side of the plate, my parents had stopped eating, a signal that it was time for

enlarged nose, his ruined complexion, his unspeakable breath. ['Whew, what a smell,' my father said.]

'Show him in,' he spluttered, pieces of toast falling from his mouth and dropping into his tumbler of gin.

---

me to be quiet. I was in no mood to take the hint by then; my future was at stake, my friends, the places where I used to play. Leaking effortlessly through our dining-room wall, Mrs Beynon's voice reached glass-shattering pitch.

'He's always got to have the last word,' my father moaned. 'That's you, that is. Your influence.'

'I hate you. BOTH of you!'

Without warning, my mother lifted the absurdly dainty cup from its saucer, its frail handle like a piece of thread between her fingers, then threw the lukewarm tea at my face. A quick jink to my left and I managed to avoid the worst of it. Apart from a splash on my shoulder, most of the tea finished up on the wallpaper, a runny map of nowhere.

'For heaven's sake, Helma,' my father whined. 'Look what you've done *now* . . .'

They were doomed to dissatisfaction from the very start. The trickle of PG Tips running down the wall my father had papered (badly) the year before was only confirmation of the fact.

'You bloody BASTARD,' my mother yelled, gritting her teeth and shaking a fist at me. Sprinting from the room, I was much too fast for either of them by then. Next door, the Beynons were quiet.

After all, I loved the house where I was born. The garden with the fishpond, the greenhouse, the shed, and, on the other side of our tall hedge, the concrete scouts' hut turning into a fortress as the years passed, with first barbed wire and then

He had long abandoned the nuances of polite behaviour, and the appearance of an upright man in military uniform at the far end of his breakfast table in no way curtailed his slurpings and chompings. The tall

---

broken bottles topping the high wall to keep vandals out. It was the area going to the dogs, my parents claimed, that decided them on the move. They needed a fresh start, a second chance to get things right. The final straw, after the graffiti, the yobbos, and the racket from the neighbours hoarding junk in their garden, had been the night a couple of kids set fire to our hedge. Alerted by laughter, my father rushed to the bedroom window one evening in time to see two boys fleeing the scene of the crime. The hedge that ran alongside the drive my parents had concreted twelve years earlier, when I was just a bump, burning like a bonfire. Not only did the fire ruin the hedge but, much worse, it threatened the car, my mother's only means of escape every summer, across the continent and back to Austria.

I don't believe my father's heart was in the move. He knew we would wind up nearer to the bad lot my mother had fallen in with, the drinkers, the smokers, but he went along with the plan, hoping it might cheer her up.

'For God's sake, Helma, there's no room in here for all this' was my father's mantra that July morning in the mid 1970s when we went to live beside the sea, near the beach where my parents met.

The move was squeezed in between my final weeks at junior school and what turned out to be my last childhood holiday in Austria. It seemed crazy to me, settling for a modern, top-floor flat when we lived in a perfectly good 1950s house that was new when they bought it. There's a photo of the two of them

figure in the medals and braid clicked his heels, nodding crisply, a mechanical man.

'We. Are very interested in. Your "Adventures". Herr von Gammon,' he said.

---

outside the front door: the proud owners, my mother wearing lipstick, my father with hair and his own teeth.

My mother, who couldn't bear to throw anything out, tried to save everything: knick-knacks; lampshades; every pair of curtains, even though we had three less windows to dress; sideboards; two nests of tables; standard lamps. My father was unhappy. Later, the bulk of it would be deposited in the attic of our new flat, piled high, left to grow a pelt of dust, but on that first day, my mother was determined to fit it all in; every snow globe, every music box.

'Listen to me, woman. There is NO ROOM. Can't you get that into your thick skull?'

Our new, boxy living-room was crammed with a leather swivel-chair and the bulgy, blue three-piece suite brought from our house in Caerethin that morning by a couple of clowns who'd questioned our move to a smaller place. The wrong scale, our furniture strained to break free, like the Incredible Hulk's muscles pushing against his white shirt.

'I told you,' I added helpfully.

My father was waist-deep in furniture, wading to the window to take another look at the view, which turned out to be a view not of the beach of their courtship but of a row of conifers. Pressing your left cheek to the window, however, you might just catch a glimpse of the sea off to the right, if the wind was westerly, parting the branches every now and again.

A rubbishy ornament in the palm of her hand, 'I hate it,' my mother whispered out of the blue, loud enough for an

'Oh yes,' said Thomas, spraying crumbs the length of the table. 'And what "Adventures" would those be?'

'Why. The "Canals". At the heart of Europe,' the officer said, surprised at this pitiful man's failure to grasp

---

eleven-year-old's ears but not for my father's. His cheek was pressed against the icy glass.

Wondering why her denunciation of our new home had been so quiet, I contemplated chipping in with a second 'See, I told you,' but something in her voice stopped me. I shouldn't push it, I thought. She's a mess. An over-elaborate Spirograph pattern. There would be moments ahead when I couldn't deal with her grief, it's true; and I can't say I'm proud of filling my ears with cotton wool while she cried herself to sleep at night, hours and hours of howling, but, slowly, just turned eleven, I was learning to shut up.

'I can see the sea!' my father chimed. 'Come and look, Steve.'

While I climbed over the chairs and sofa to join him, my mother disappeared into their new bedroom, where the removal men had left our record player, and, as I struggled to see what my father could see, waves breaking on the beach a mile from home, the music began.

. . . *ree-d'Ee-dee-o, dee ree-d'Ee-dee-o* . . .

'Oh, Dad . . .' I wheedled. 'Tell her! She's so . . . churlish.'

My father looked up to the sky, all but obscured by conifers, and groaned without even acknowledging my new word.

'Jesus Christ,' he said softly . . . *dee ree-d'Ee-dee-o.* . . and then 'FOR GOD'S SAKE, CAN'T YOU GIVE IT A REST?' making me jump.

. . . *ree-d'Ee-dee-o, dee ree-d'Ee-dee-o* . . .

'You go,' my father said. 'I can't talk to her.'

Her head in her hand, my mother was hunched on the edge

the purpose of his visit, though his training forbade him to show even a flicker of disdain. 'The War,' he said. 'There is a War.'

Von Gammon, who had already lost his eldest son to

---

of their queen-size bed. It so filled the room that her knees touched the dressing-table. With so little space, the record player, a present to my father for twenty-five years with British Steel, sat at the head of the bed, their four, fat pillows pushed to one side.

'Don't,' I said. 'It's not fair.'

When I sat on the mattress beside her, the extra weight upset the balance, and the stylus skittered across the record, a horrible unzipping that made me jump away from my mother, afraid that her hand would swing out to slosh me one on the side of the face.

'Sorry.'

Nothing happened. She didn't move. Then the music resumed where the needle had stopped, a track as maudlin as the one she was listening to when she began crying.

. . . *ree-d'Ee-dee-o, dee ree-d'Ee-dee-o . . . dee ree-d'Ee-dee-o* . . . They all sounded the same to me.

Despite her years in Wales she was an Austrian through and through. There were always worse days to come, until the nadir, when she began to mix alcohol with the Valium and Mogadon prescribed by our GP, a genial chap who struggled with her accent.

She stood up in the hairdresser's one day, complaining of a pain in her head, then proceeded to rub and rub her cranium, erasing her half-completed perm. In 'a terrible state', the hairdresser's girl said afterwards, when my father turned up in a flap.

the conflict, had forbidden all talk of the war in his presence and, on hearing it at that moment, hurled a coffee pot at the soldier who dared to raise this taboo subject in his presence. Neatly side-stepping the missile,

---

'Oh dear, oh dear, oh dear, oh dear . . .' she muttered, pacing the salon, shuffling through the locks of grey and white hair (she was one of their younger customers) while the girl brewed a cup of tea.

'Two sugars, is it?'

The other customers, imprisoned under giant hairdryers, aliens with enormous brains, and a little deaf anyway, absorbed the household tips in their magazines, accustomed to the agitated giant among them.

'Oh dear, oh dear, oh dear. No sugar, thank you. Sweeteners.'

The drone of the machines was awful, she told me later, drilling into her head.

'Best have some sugar, is it?'

From then on, she found it difficult to sleep. In my teenage years, we played more games of Scrabble in the dead of night than I can remember – patiently laying out the tiles, totting up the score, rummaging in the plastic bag for fresh letters, a routine to keep her mind occupied, to stop her pacing, her muttering, her anxious moments. Unconnected words connected in every direction as we tried to reach all four corners of the board.

'Thank you,' she would whisper, at the end of a game I had won by miles, while the sun was smudging our picture window with grey, slowly, the conifers reappearing; trunks, branches, needles. My father's snores leaked through the wall to reach us, in the living room, as I poured the letters back into their bag. 'Thank you.'

the officer continued to talk as if nothing had happened.

'We believe your canals could be. Invaluable. In our glorious "Struggle". Invaluable to. "Exterminate" the enemy. Exterminate them all!'

Did our long, low-scoring games of Scrabble come after the half-hearted suicide attempt, or before? The diaries I kept back then were burnt years ago, without so much as a second glance at their woeful entries, the unrequited love and the lists of favourite films alongside my mother's 'turns'. Perhaps it happened before we moved, before she fell to pieces, before she was utterly maddened by grief.

... *ree-d'Ee-dee-o, dee ree-d'Ee-dee-o* ...

Was there music playing? There usually was, and the old bedroom I ran into seems bigger, in my memory, than the one in the top-floor flat; lighter, airier, untouched by the worst of her doleful presence.

... *ree-d'Ee-dee-o, dee ree-d'Ee-dee-o* ...

Did I even run? Perhaps I popped upstairs to check on her. Was she still sobbing or was she asleep? When I found her on the edge of the bed, the neat, white candlewick bedspread, a glass of water on the white bedside cabinet, her mouth full of little white pills I scooped from her mouth. I didn't know what they were, but she was taking too many. She coughed and spluttered, demanding I stop but offering no resistance, heavy in my arms.

... *ree-d'Ee-dee-o, dee ree-d'Ee-dee-o* ...

'Lay down. Lay down.'

There had already been so many days and nights of tears, of music played too long and too loud, of her body stretched out on the bed, immobile, her puffy face, her useless hands, her endless sobbing in German – words impossible to make

It took a great deal of arguing, achingly slow cajoling, wooden flattery and diplomacy to persuade von Gammon to reveal the precise location of his discovery of fifteen years earlier.

---

out though I could guess at their meaning – that I must have been inured to her misery by then, a cold and practical boy.

. . . *ree-d'Ee-dee-o, dee ree-d'Ee-dee-o . . .*

So, scraping a handful of pills off her tongue and throwing them on the floor or against the white wall, where they rattled like hailstones, was just another episode in her long decline from greatness. Ozymandias, two vast and trunkless legs.

Her reliance on music as a soundtrack for her grief lessened over time or was, mercifully, varied by melancholy numbers from the charts, Queen or Demis Roussos temporarily usurping the yodellers, until plants took all her attention. Within weeks of arriving in our new flat, every window-sill was crowded with pot-plants. Busy Lizzies, rubber plants, ferns, cacti, a huge yucca tree in one corner pushing against the low ceiling, dwarfing even my mother, let alone my father, who picked his way around 'this ruddy jungle' like Stanley. Anything that would grow indoors, in fact. Leaves of all shapes and sizes monopolized the light.

'Oi, Bertha, you're confusing the birds with all this nonsense,' my father said the afternoon a fourth sparrow flew smack into our window, fluttering, like Hermann, two floors down to the pocket garden outside our ground-floor neighbour's flat. Still on the damp earth. This was always happening on rainy days.

'Don't talk rubbish,' my mother muttered, her fingers pushing down the soil in a plant-pot, readying it for a seedling. Broken nails, her skin cracked and stained by the earth, the pads of her fingers rough again, as they must have been when

197

[Although it was just the sort of stuff to have sent me to sleep, this was the kind of detail my father skated over. In the end, it was the chance to avenge the death of his beloved son that convinced Thomas von Gammon to unearth the journal, charts and drawings he had locked away years before.]

---

she played the zither, but surprisingly delicate for all that.

I was dispatched downstairs to see if the creature was still alive. Usually, it wasn't, and twice I carried weightless bodies to the nearby golf links to bury them in the rough, overlooking the sea.

She missed her garden in the old house. Not the chance to sunbathe – she could do that in the field at the back of the flats, and did until she shone like a magnificent piece of mahogany furniture – but her vegetable patch, her cold frame, our sweet, miniature greenhouse-tomatoes. She waited five years for one of the allotments on the slope below Oystermouth castle to become available, her name floating to the top of the waiting list one afternoon in the early 1980s. A strip of land the previous tenant had neglected, it was taken away from him and handed to my mother, whom the committee could tell was, even in her reduced state, clothes hanging off her, skin loose, very much up to the task. She was only too willing to spend whole days digging, weeding, planting, or making windmills from Fairy Liquid bottles to scare away the birds. If Austria called when she was out, my father had been instructed to say 'Heli is in the *Schreber*garden'. Returning home red-faced, dirty, she complained of exhaustion, but couldn't wait to go back the following day

'What's the matter with you, woman?' my father would

With the help of two engineers – Jules Verne and Edgar Rice Burroughs – the Austrian Navy began the excavations of vast shafts that would enable them to lower a fleet of dreadnoughts to the heart of Europe. Weeks of intensive labour began on two fronts, the miners preparing the shaft, and builders in the shipyards creating powerful warships suitable for subterranean sailing, narrow craft with searchlights capable of penetrating any darkness.

'Hup, hup, hup,' an officer yapped.

---

demand (he told me this, I had long since moved away), and she would shrug. 'Can't you get it through your thick skull? Don't dig for so long.'

'You can't tell your mother anything,' he'd say on the phone, as puzzled as ever, a lack of German the least of his problems.

'If it makes her happy,' I'd reply, as confused as he was.

It must have. If not the work itself, the hours stooping over the earth, pulling weeds, digging, her hands blistered, her perm unpicked by the wind, then the opportunity to itemize, over dinner, the food on our plate that she'd grown herself, pointing at each vegetable in turn, as I raised them to my mouth.

'That's from my garden ... That's from my garden ... *And* that ... Do you like the carrots/potatoes/lettuce/radishes?'

There was always too much piled on my plate, and my mother was always at my shoulder, serving herself last of all, ready to give me more, while I grumbled ungraciously about the Third World or putting on weight, though nothing was left at the end of the meal.

'Hup, hup, hup,' the engineers replied, hoisting a giant girder for the tunnel into place.

'Hup, hup, hup,' an officer yapped.

'Hup, hup, hup,' the engineers replied, hoisting a giant funnel for a battleship into place.

When, a year after the visit of the Dalek officer, the strategy of steaming beneath the trenches to outflank the enemy was ready for implementation, Thomas von Gammon insisted on being aboard the flagship.

'I muft go,' he muttered, a poor creature who had lost the use of the letter S.

'Muft you?' his wife replied in solidarity.

'Yef,' he said.

'Well, if you muft.' His wife, who did not want to lose a husband as she had lost a son, was, nevertheless, pleased to see him go. The thought of breakfasting without his sulkiness for a few weeks proved irresistible, not to mention fresh sheets and the bed all to herself.[23] The opportunity to rediscover the letter S was almost as inviting.

'Goodbye, my darling,' she said, kissing him demurely on both cheeks. 'Have a fafe journey.'

She watched from a platform especially constructed

23. My grandfather was the first to die, in June 1973, the year my mother returned with the music box. She was closest to her father, and the shock of his death was delayed, only to spread over the years, a terrible inkblot blackening everything,

for the wives and families of departing sailors, as his ship was lowered on gigantic pulleys into the seemingly bottomless shaft, the mighty roar of the winches drowning out her final words as she waved to him, blowing kisses he was too distracted to return. The groan of metal on metal contorted the faces of loved ones on either side of her as they bade farewell to their brave boys, the reminder of chalk on a blackboard too much to bear for those who had always hated school.

['Silly people,' my father was quick to add.]

It was the last time Mrs von Gammon ever saw her husband, and, fearing a loss of morale during the war, there was very little speculation in the press regarding the fate of the ships and their crews.

EXPLORER OFF ON ONE LAST ADVEN-TURE was the first bold headline, above a story about the war effort from a scientific angle, and then, two weeks later, buried on an inside page, in the smallest type available:

Explorer not heard from.

To this day, many stories are told of what happened

---

inch by inch, so troubled was she by his disappointment, the sadness he felt when his only girl failed to return home to Austria after her year in Britain.

'*Bitte . . . bitte . . . bitte . . .*' she cried, over and over, stretched out on the bed, drunk, begging his forgiveness, 'Please . . .'

A communist family, we were atheists. So, with no hope of

on that fateful mission on the underground canals of Europe. Some say they reached France only to find that the French, anticipating a sneak attack and already aware of the mazy caverns and conduits, had stationed their own fleet to lie in wait for the Austrian Navy, sinking it without warning.

Another variation suggests that the fleet – hopelessly lost in the uncharted, subterranean waters – is sailing to this day, unable to find a way back to the surface, and that what's left of the crews are now in their nineties, doddery, asthmatic sailors surviving on a diet of fungus (scraped from the sides of the cavern walls) supplemented by the strange, eyeless fish they catch with makeshift rods.

Some say they developed their own underground culture, unique in all the world.

Cavern operas, with music written to take unusual acoustics into account.

Mysterious sculptures inspired by the formation of stalactites and stalagmites.

---

an afterlife where she might meet her father again, she was inconsolable. Years later, she told me about her mother's death. Perhaps this was the harder of the two bereavements to take, to cope with guilt at the death of the parent you feel, deep down, you should have loved more or better.

In the February of 1974, she was called by Hari in the middle of the night. By then, she was frightened of the telephone ringing at odd hours, early in the morning or late in the evening.

A poetry of scraps of paper, tickets, receipts and diaristic jottings that dwells on images of light and wind and the changing seasons.

Ballets that move to the rhythms of dripping water.

Long novels of life above ground, works that lovingly record domestic life, full of the kind of banalities most of us take for granted — journeys to the shops, involved descriptions of meals with loved ones, the leather patch on the elbow of a jacket, the drawer in the kitchen that held life's bits and bobs, the needles, screws, and pieces of thread.

I prefer the more gruesome version my father told me.

They sail for three days and three nights, trusting their erratic compasses, singing martial songs, until they hear, far off, a noise.

MMMMMMMMMMMMMMMMMMMMMMMMMMMMMMMMMMMMMMMMMMMMMMMMMMMMMMMMMMMMMMMMM

MMMMMMMMMMMMMMMMMMMMMMMMMMMMMMMMMMMMMMMMMMMMMMMMMMMMMMMMMMMMMMMMM

MMMMMMMMMMMMMMMMMMMMMMMMMMMMMMMMMMMMMMMMMMMMMMMMMMMMMMMMMMMMMMMMM

My mother booked the first available flight. Distracted, unable to organize herself, she rambled incoherently, paying more for the journey than we could afford. My father helped her to pack enough warm clothes for a week. We never travelled to Austria in the winter, when ordinary families holidayed there, so I knew things must be serious.

There was so much snow — blackening clouds, smothering roads and burying fields, chalets deep in snow, cars up to their

```
MMMMMMMMMMMMMMMMMMMMMMMMMMMMMMMMMMMMMM
MMMMMMMMMMMMMMMMMMMMMMMMMMMMMMMMMMMMMM
MMMMMMMMMMMMMMMMMMMMMMMMMMMMMMMMMMMMMM
MMMMMMMMMMMMMMMMMMMMMMMMMMMMMMMMMMMMM
MMMMMMMMMMMMMMMMMMMMMMMMMMMMMMMMMMMM
MMMMMMMMMMMMMMMMMMMMMMMMMMMMMMMMMMM
MMMMMMMMMMMMMMMMMMMMMMMMMMMMMMMMMM
MMMMMMMMMMMMMMMMMMMMMMMMMMMMMMMMM
MMMMMMMMMMMMMMMMMMMMMMMMMMMMMMMM
MMMMMMMMMMMMMMMMMMMMMMMMMMMMMMM
MMMMMMMMMMMMMMMMMMMMMMMMMMMMMM
MMMMMMMMMMMMMMMMMMMMMMMMMMMMM
MMMMMMMMMMMMMMMMMMMMMMMMMMMM
MMMMMMMMMMMMMMMMMMMMMMMMMMM
MMMMMMMMMMMMMMMMMMMMMMMMMM
MMMMMMMMMMMMMMMMMMMMMMMMM
MMMMMMMMMMMMMMMMMMMMMMMM
```

---

necks in it – so much snow where she was heading that her
flight from Heathrow was delayed, then, once in the air, prevented from landing. The aeroplane circled the airport. Below
her, teams of men and machines worked to clear the runways.

Too young, of course, I never saw the hospital where my
grandmother spent her last days, the hospital my mother was
rushing to because her brother had told her she had to come
at once, the one my brother described to me years later as a
small building a short walk from the centre of Knittelfeld (but,
if you lived abroad, like my mother, too far away). At one time,
he told me, it must have been in green fields, although, by 1974,

MMMMMMMMMMMMMMMMMMMMMM
MMMMMMMMMMMMMMMMMMMMMM
MMMMMMMMMMMMMMMMMMMMMM
MMMMMMMMMMMMMMMMMMM.

The hum becomes a drone, then a roaring they might have mistaken for thunder were it not for the fact that no sounds from the outside world can reach them where they are.

By the time they realize they are sailing in an ever-strengthening current pulling them closer and closer towards the terrifying roar, it is too late to turn back.

The rumble grows and grows like a threat of doom, like the voice of God.

Thomas von Gammon and his fellow sailors can see, ahead of them, picked out by the powerful searchlights, plumes of smoke rising to the roof of the cavern, billowing up like fumes from Hell.

---

the urban sprawl had caught up with the place, surrounded by pre-war houses and flats, the grounds in the shade of tall linden trees.

Now, with my brother's help, I can place our mother there, out of breath, hours later than she should have been, walking down the long, blank corridors – she daren't run here, not in a hospital – her shoes clicking on shiny floors, in the thick of visiting hour, the visitors moving sluggishly around her like a stream thickened with ice, but our mother is an astronaut, too slow, why can't she move any quicker? Heading for the first floor and the ward where her mother is waiting, she passes

'It is over,' Thomas von Gammon mutters to himself. 'My journey is at an end.'

Unlike that fateful day or night (he never knew which) sixteen years earlier, when he had slid on his backside towards the centre of the earth until his bottom was almost showing, these really are his final words.

Pulled inexorably forward, the crews of the *Zeltweg*, the *Dachstein*, and the *Großglockner* see, at last, what confronts them.

Not smoke from the flames of Hell but a mighty waterfall greater than any on the surface of the planet, a waterfall that drops miles beneath them, a waterfall with clouds of vapour capable of blotting out an entire country

---

a doctor carrying a syringe, he's wearing a long white coat discoloured by handprints, the colour of the cream walls, she walks to the ward where her mother is dying, tiny now amidst all this activity, the trolleys and the nurses and the nuns and the visitors, she walks (shrunken now, a little girl), walks to the ward where the nurses have been pleased on the days there was no sign of glucose in her mother's urine – her mother diabetic as well as crippled by a stroke – though she can't speak clearly and she cries all the time, catheterized, though still her bed is wet and, here and there, bloodstained, her medical insurance all gone, which is why the physiotherapy and the measuring of blood glucose have stopped, and my mother's shoes are made of lead as she moves, in slow motion, down the blank, dark corridor, to the dingy ward where her

bigger than Wales, a country the size of Austria, a waterfall that plunges so far and so darkly beneath them that they are unable to see the bottom even as they plummet towards it.

They have hours and hours to contemplate their fate, long enough to write final notes no one will ever read.

A cold wind howls through the portholes and the funnels, singing a song no one on board ever wanted to hear.

A cold wind plucks rivets from their holes like fruit.

A cold wind whistles forlornly through the cabins where last letters from wives and sweethearts dance on the ceiling like confetti.

Down they go, drawn by the terrible law of gravity.

---

mother is waiting, the blinds drawn, her eyes wide because it must be dark, so dark all along the corridor where her leaden feet are carrying her, so slowly, to her mother in a ward upstairs, dying, waiting for her daughter to arrive, her daughter, climbing stairs, apologizing to a nurse she recognizes, sorry that she's late, the doors swing open to the ward, the blinds are drawn, the lights on although it isn't late, *ich kann nicht verstehen*, and then the bed, the small bed where her mother died, it must have been minutes earlier – while her daughter entered the hospital, while she squeezed past visitors along the corridor? – died before her daughter could arrive in time to say anything, to say goodbye, or sorry – '*Bitte* . . .' – to say anything at all, her daughter frozen still.

The sheets still warm; a rosary; a glass of water; the one pillow dented like snow.

7·

OTTO

Count Otto von Otto, First Admiral of the Austrian Fleet, an excellent swimmer who can hold his breath underwater for ten minutes, is sent by his Government to sabotage the Turkish Armada in the Bosphorus. It is the 1840s: Marx has just completed his stint as editor of *Rheinische Zeitung*, Engels is about to publish *The Condition of the Working Classes in England*, the crinoline is coming in, and there is tension in the Balkans.

One of the Austro-Hungarian Empire's great sailors, Count Otto, is standing on the shores of that treacherous expanse of water whose opposing currents make it extremely turbulent. Bursts of white foam explode from the syrupy, black waves. Fish take shelter under rocks. Behind enemy lines, Otto is flanked by a crack team in discreet military dress. It is dark despite a three-quarters moon and his saboteurs are barely visible against the louring crags of the Bulgarian coastline. Only the Count's chestful of gold medals catch what little light there is. (Several kilos in weight, they represent a selection of Otto's campaign trophies, accumulated over the years of an illustrious career, displayed in a giant cabinet[24] back home, in his Viennese townhouse). They glint in the moonlight like ghostly tears as he beckons his second-in-command, a young, unusually tall man who will die of a broken heart in his tenth decade on hearing of the outbreak of the Great War, mourning his advanced years, frustrated that he will not be able to die for his country; which, in a manner of speaking, he does after all.

24. Returning from Obdach, flustered by our hectic schedule, overheated, we found Günther in the garden. West of his unpopulated fishpond, dressed only in a pair of white briefs, he was on his knees painting a pole of his clothes-line fire-engine green before the rain. He stood to wave, his tanned skin burnished by the sun, a perfect advertisement for Kundl's laundering skills. Those dazzling underpants!

'Did you clear your room this morning?' my mother asked as we settled down, our places already laid for us, three raffia mats, three spoons, three knives and forks, my father struggling to slide his legs under the table. 'Kundl goes in that room every second Sunday.'

I remembered my dream at the lake: Kundl delving beneath the bed, her hand, clutching a lemon duster, reaching for my suitcase. I decided that it was now or never.

'No,' I said. 'I'll pop upstairs when we've eaten.'

Shuttling between the oven, the cupboards and the table, Kundl greeted us without pausing in her chores, her face flushed from the activity, no sign that she'd discovered anything. Günther bellowed what might have been an instruction, though almost everything my uncle said could have been a command.

'Isn't he eating with us?' I asked.

'We go tonight,' Count Otto whispers, his voice like thunder.

'You should know the Mödritschers by now,' my father said, grinning like a man who knows he's always right. 'Oh yes.'

While Günther's head bobbed outside the kitchen window, Kundl served the meal alone, despite my mother's offers of help, beginning with a clear soup, two *Knödel* soaking like doughy icebergs. My mother muttered, 'She could have warmed it a bit more,' just as Günther, his head through the open window, demanded to know how everything was.

'*Wunderbar!*' my father called.

Our noises of approval rumbled like the approaching storm. We helped ourselves to seconds, Kundl hovering beside us with the saucepan and a serving spoon.

'*Nein danke*, Kundl,' my father said. '*Genug ist genug!*'

My mother was already struggling, cursing the sausage she'd eaten in Obdach, but she was determined to soldier on, taking an ostentatiously deep breath between every mouthful of soup, loosening the belt of her summer dress by a single notch. She was, I'm sure, a little afraid of her older brother, who would have stormed in, tyrannically hospitable, insisting she tell him what was wrong with his food, and wasn't it good enough for his English sister? (Always English, never Welsh. On the rare occasions he wrote to his sister, the envelopes were addressed *Swansea, Wales, England.*)

Kundl replaced our soup dishes with plates of runny mushroom goulash surmounted by another dumpling, and, while my mother explained how one should never cut the dumpling in the goulash with a knife, always a spoon, because using a knife would be to imply it was under-cooked, the smell of

Among the brave marines, monocles fall from eyes.

Günther's paint wafted through to us on a breath of air. As all our breathing deepened and the whites of our plates came into view like a sighting of land, Günther shouted from the garden. Moments later, he entered, his underpants the makings of a Jackson Pollock canvas, and rooted in the cupboards as though there were a bomb planted somewhere in the kitchen. A strand of slicked hair dropped in front of his face as he rose from one cupboard with a bottle of schnapps he was determined we should sample.

'*Jo, Heli. Komm.*'

'*Ein Bissel,*' my mother replied.

Kundl, requiring a few insistent words from my mother before she agreed, as though her place was in the servant's quarters, sat down to join us for this drink. My mother said something to Günther. He shrugged then filled a fifth shot-glass with a schnapps made from pine cones. It smelled of toilet disinfectant. We drank to the chef, Günther – who stood beside us, nodding at our raised glasses – and his assistant, Kundl, perching awkwardly on the bench-seat next to my father.

'VERY GOOD,' my father enunciated to Kundl, who wasn't in the least bit deaf. She nodded once and smiled.

The toast completed, Kundl began to clear away the dishes, running water in the sink while Günther marched back out as though the washing-line had called him to demand another coat of paint.

We didn't spend much more than forty-five minutes at the table, the time it took Günther to finish painting the two metal poles. As we left the kitchen, my parents for a lie down at Hari's before Seckau, and me to my task, Kundl bowed.

'Aber . . .'

_____

Upstairs, I struggled with my suitcase. It took two hands and all my strength to pull it from under the bed, and I wondered how my elderly father had lifted it, let alone managed the walk from the car and into Günther's house with it on the day I arrived.

'Jesus CHRIST!' I muttered involuntarily, sounding more like Dad than I ever could when trying to parody him.

It was a mad enterprise, trying to put things back the way they were, to undo the years of sentimental kleptomania, to act as if my wounded mother, stretched out on the bed, had issued instructions all those years ago, pleading *'Bitte. . . früher war eus besser . . .'* but, I reasoned, I had come this far.

It was difficult enough, foraging in my parents' attic to find every piece of bric-à-brac she had taken from Günther's house over the years, though I knew she wouldn't miss anything from the attic. Smuggling what had survived out of the flat while they were shopping was surprisingly easy; there was less than I remembered. So many objects had disintegrated under the accumulated weight of photographic equipment, *Captain Scarlet* annuals, toys, school exercise-books, and back numbers of *Amateur Photographer*. Paying the excess baggage to carry it back to Austria was an inconvenience, but that's all. Creeping around the shelves and cabinets with an armful of souvenirs while my uncle and Kundl prowled downstairs was tricky, but not impossible.

I unloaded: the twenty-year-old calendars; the snowing globe of the Prater in Vienna with a third of its water leaked away and hardly any snowflakes left to make a decent storm; five ugly satyrs my uncle had brought back from Greece; ancient

The Count will hear nothing of their doubts. Are they not officers of the Austrian Fleet, sworn to uphold the honour of the Empire?

———————

manuals for a washing machine, a food mixer, and a central-heating system; books given to my uncle by his parents inscribed with my grandfather's wrought handwriting; a paper-weight with an anchor inside (the symbol of the insurance company that Günther used to work for); and the music box that played the tune my grandmother sang in the Swansea pub when my mother wasn't there. I'd arranged them neatly, with tissue paper wedged between everything, packed them the way my mother taught me how to pack a case for leaving home. Nothing was broken.

They were a strange history. Their appearances charted my growth through childhood, adolescence and into adulthood: my puzzlement when I found the music box that made my parents shout; a year later, the snowing globe from my uncle's desk that couldn't have been a gift, it didn't look new enough; and then the instruction manuals that finally gave the game away, my bafflement turning to shame, so much shame that I didn't dare invite my friends to our house, afraid they might question the accumulation of objects on our shelves and window-sills, not that they would have dared accept an invitation.

Gift, by the by, is German for 'poison'.

By the time I was fourteen, so many objects cluttered our home that the place resembled a tatty museum, hopeless souvenirs three deep on the sills, peeping out from among the foliage, gathering dust in every corner, until, one afternoon, my father (who had had enough) shoved them in boxes, banishing them to the attic like Mrs Rochester.

'I will lead.'

'I've just about had enough of you, madam,' he said, slapping his palms together to remove the dirt. A job well done and no hands raised in anger.

I had brought with me to Austria a couple of photographs from my father's vast, uncatalogued collection. Both of Günther's living room, they were the best chance I had of replacing the items exactly where they'd stood twenty years before. In one, my mother sits on her brother's expensive leather sofa, flanked by her mother and father, a watery smile leaking from her face. Her father's smile. To their left, on top of the television, stand a couple of the satyrs. In the second photograph, my mother and father beam at the camera together, a broad smile from my mother this time, so perhaps she'd had a drink, though, to judge from the late 1960s fashions, before drink was a problem. The snow globe is on a shelf to their right, and the paperweight is there, beside the music box. I wondered when my uncle had noticed their absence, or, indeed, if he ever had.

When I'd left them downstairs, Kundl was at the sink, up to her wrists in soapy water, and Günther had disappeared into his shed with the pot of paint and the brush, bellowing operatically. The curtains drawn, the door shut, I moved around the dark living room, listening for footsteps on the stairs, convinced that I could finish the task uninterrupted. My uncle must eat, after all, and his underpants weren't so stained with paint that he needed to change. I had placed the satyrs on the TV set beside their replacements, two golden elephants, imagining Günther noticing them months later; perplexed, outraged maybe, but glad to have them back.

I was busily tucking the white-goods manuals into the bottom

So, marching into the tepid sea they wade towards the guns of the Ottoman Fleet, clustered half a mile offshore. The deceptively calm waters knock at sturdy bows.

Aboard their ships, the Turks are sleeping soundly, the ratings blotto, their officers tipsy from too many kegs of wine. Little do they suspect that even while they snore, dreaming of home, their fate is to be decided by the plucky

---

of a drawer, beneath a stack of soiled TV guides, when the door opened.

In paint-stained pants, the Baron stood in the doorway. As big as the door. No more than splinters of light behind him. He was looking from me, head down in a drawer, to the collection of possessions on the coffee table – objects he hadn't seen for years, gifts from his parents for the most part – then looking back again, to my hand holding the instruction manual for a washing machine he'd dispensed with a decade ago.

Both of us blocks of ice.

'*Ich habe . . .*' I mumbled. '*Es war mich . . . Diese . . . Diesem . . .*' (nominative, accusative, or dative, was all I could think) '*Sache sind . . .*' (my vocabulary was as bad then as when I'd all but failed my German A-level thirteen summers earlier) '. . . returned . . . *Sein . . . Seine . . . Deine . . .*'

I couldn't even take the blame for my mother's actions. Closing the drawer, I waited for my uncle's voice to climb its register, for Kundl to rush upstairs, a dishcloth in her fist, to find out what she'd done wrong this time.

Silently – to this day, I have no explanation, though he might just have understood what was going on, there was always that chance – my uncle closed the door.

Austrians, Otto's men, who slowly disappear beneath the waves, synchronously kicking their legs.

'*Links, recht, links, recht, links, recht . . .*'

First the water is at their chests, lapping at Count Otto's medals, making even heavier the heavy serge uniforms, then it is at their necks, and then with a final, mighty inhalation they go under. If the Turkish sailors had been alert now and scanning the shore, all they would have seen was a phalanx of spikes poking out of the sea, moving determinedly towards their destiny, wonderful swimmers to a man.[25]

25. I wouldn't claim to be a wonderful swimmer, but Austria was where I learnt to swim, in the outdoor municipal pool, when I was eight; by then, too old for my father's tales of the Austrian Navy.

On my second day back, my mother drove me around the town to visit my childhood haunts, collecting me from Günther's, my father stepping out of the car to greet me like a gentleman, dapper in white slacks and a short-sleeved shirt that showed off the loose skin ruched at his elbows. I sat in the back, moving from side to side as the buildings went by.

'*Maßweger Straße, Sachendorfer Gasse*, the *Lindenallee* . . . You remember this, Stefan.'

In the driving seat, conducting us from place to place, my mother was enjoying herself, enjoying her home town, as if seeing it for the first time, looking around to check my reaction.

'Keep your eyes on the road, Fred,' my father groaned, 'or you'll get us killed.'

We crawled around the town, never going over fifteen miles

The seven marines breast-stroked towards the enemy in an arrowhead formation, the Count at their head, leading by example.

[At this point my father would pull a determined face, becoming Count Otto undaunted by the water's blackness, holding his breath at the foot of my bed. And I was with him, trying not to breathe but failing, amazed at the capacity of Teutonic lungs yet willing to give my father the benefit of the doubt.]

---

an hour, past guest-houses, past the hatchet-faced supermarket, then into the centre, two roads running parallel – neither much longer than a sprinting track – the town beige, a toy town. Just off the main square, a railway engine was mounted on a plinth like a kill. We drove past family businesses, butchers, boutiques, shoe shops with footwear at least a decade out of fashion, and the toy shops I remembered nagging my parents to visit, where the most exciting thing on display was still a box of coloured pencils.

Heading back to the Lindenallee and my grandparents' last home, we passed the swimming pool I was taken to at least twice a week during the holiday; sometimes by my parents, more often by my cousin Lianne.

'Can we stop here?' I asked.

The approach to the pool was familiar but the building itself had changed, the pebble-dash walls smoothed over and covered by a mural of distorted, hippyish figures snaking around one another, enveloping a variety of flowers with psychedelically vivid petals.

At the turnstile, my mother slipped into the role of translator she would so much enjoy that week, chatting to the

Reaching the finest of the vessels, the flagship bedecked with bunting, silks and gold leaf, the Austrians peal from their formation, positioning themselves in a line along the keel. At a signal from the Count, they kick their flippered feet, the only concession to their aquatic

---

attendant in the glass booth at the entrance while my father remained in the car, nursing his inhaler. My mother was recognized as a Mödritscher by the woman at the gate, so, after a few words of conversation – who was living, who had died – we were allowed to look round without paying. Proof, for my mother, that there were still good people left in the world.

That cloudy afternoon, there were only a handful of swimmers. Those entering the water did so with scarcely a ripple, leaving the surface to reflect the sky and the trees at the far end of the pool, which, bordered by a low wire fence, was open to the countryside.

Almost everything inside was as it was: a stepped slope down to the water, where people towelled themselves dry then sunbathed on wooden, slatted racks; the rows of changing rooms at either side of the entrance, with Wild West saloon-doors; the glass-walled canteen where I bought my bottles of Fanta and Afri-Cola; the pebbles set into the concrete paths hurting my bare feet, making me walk as if the floor was on fire, which, on the hottest summer days, it was.

'There used to be a diving board at one end of the pool, didn't there?' I asked, knowing, of course, that there was. 'A springboard and a concrete high-board.'

At least once a visit, I'd inch to the edge of the high board to peer over, contemplating that drop to the turquoise water

activities, impaling the ship on their helmets' spikes.

The vessel is fatally holed!

The wood groans in pain and, on board, six little jets of water spring from the hold like drinking fountains.

Why only six? Because disaster has struck. Count Otto von Otto's *pickelhaube* is stuck fast and he is unable to withdraw it.

As with all great men, he has a fatal flaw. In some it is ambition, in others it is greed, for the Count it is vanity and always knowing what's best. Having insisted that his spike should be at least two centimetres longer than anyone else's, Count Otto now finds those extra centimetres imperiling his life. He is faced with the thought that he might never see his beloved homeland again, his favourite

---

miles below; never daring to jump but swearing that one day I would.

'They got rid of them years ago,' my mother sighed, taking it personally. 'It's a shame.'

The platform had been replaced by a small, sky-blue water-chute that couldn't represent an unconquerable fear for any child, which was all right by me.

'Dad taught me to swim here when I was eight.'

Beside me in the deep end, he let the air out of my rubber ring without telling me – an imperceptible ripple of breath at my side. I floated as I had floated all that summer, held up, I believed, by the yellow and orange tube of air, until he pointed out that I was swimming.

mountain, the lake he would visit when he was looking for a little bit of peace and quiet.[26]

[My father went 'Glug, glug, glug.']

Otto struggles to break free, kicking his legs and thrashing his arms, but he cannot loosen the spike, so the ship is stuck to his head like one of Carmen Miranda's more outrageous hats.

In the murky waters of the Bosphorus, his stout companions fail to notice their leader's predicament. They

---

26. 'Couldn't this keep till tomorrow?' I asked, knowing it wouldn't.

On my first day back, grumpy from Vienna airport, I was taken straight from Günther's tour of his desolate house to my parents' favourite lake.

'It isn't late,' my mother said.

That depended on which clock you consulted. Though the one on the dashboard had been set to Austrian time, my mother never touched her wristwatch after leaving Wales. She couldn't decide where she wanted to be.

It was late afternoon but the sun was still warm for our twenty-minute drive to the Ingeringsee, at the foot of the Seckau mountains, past miles of pine forest, photogenic rivers and farmland with no sign of animals, not even shit. Trees standing on either side of flattened trunks, as if Christo had organized an advertisement for Gillette, only a swathe of cleared forest showed evidence of human activity.

We rolled to a halt in a gravelly spot at the edge of a forest, alongside the only other car. The handbrake crunched into position. Cooler at the lake, it was eerily quiet (abandoned, haunted), the sun dazzling as I squinted to a point where the

swim to the next ship, waving their froggy feet in time, a military precision their drowning leader would have been proud to behold.

Only Count Otto remains stuck, his eyes popping like a trumpeter's, his lungs close to bursting, the claustrophobic

---

path through the woods disappeared into shadow. While my father unpacked his camera-case from the boot, my mother was fussing, excited to have me there, still in the shorts she'd worn that morning at the airport. The material strained across her thighs, showing off her varicose veins, though that never bothered her.

'Do you want to borrow a cardigan?' my mother asked.

We walked into the shadows, along a woodland path, a gentle incline to the water's edge, though my father, as usual, was trailing, as frail as Francis Chichester back from sailing around the world. He didn't complain at being left behind, but there was a look of concentration on his face, a couple of creases at the bridge of his nose, more obvious because he had removed his sunglasses to study the path ahead of him.

'Do you come up here every holiday?' I asked, dropping back to relieve him of the camera-case.

It was heavier than it appeared, squashy leather loaded with lenses and coloured filters, a light meter, a flash-gun, and the book of instructions; expensive equipment he'd bought long before railway modelling became his hobby. It was rarely used after this change of interests, but he continued to lug the shoulder-bag around with him anyway, even though the only thing he ever used was the pocket-sized camera.

'At some point we do, yes,' he said.

It was as good a way to measure the passing years as any,

dark unbearable, the pressure unbearable. It seems as if everything is lost.

Just when he thinks he is about to drown, Otto sees his trusty second-in-command gliding towards him through the gloom, a bayonet in his hand and a determined

---

that walk to the Ingeringsee every summer. The time it took to reach the lake a little longer every year, the distance to the water a little more difficult every summer. He was breathing heavily through pursed lips, as if cooling a hot drink, his dewlap trembling with every exhalation.

'You can't fish here!' my mother called back as we passed a sign nailed to an evergreen. 'You'll get a heavy fine if they catch you.'

'Do you notice how clean it is?' my father said.

We ambled around the lake, the still waters showing the mountain its face, looking for the bench where my father had photographed my mother ten years earlier, when (she told us) she was happy. The photo hung on the wall in my parents' flat in Swansea. Blown up to the size of a small table and mounted in a clip-frame, it captured my mother sitting with Christl (then still her sister-in-law) in front of a panoramic view of the Ingeringsee, though it wasn't the view but one another they were facing. Gossiping, no doubt, or discussing the cost of dentistry.

A few years after the print was given pride of place on the wall above the television, it began to pucker behind the glass, the result of cheap glue and DIY framing. Soon after that, Christl began proceedings to divorce my Uncle Helmut, though this wasn't a parallel my parents would have drawn. Hadn't *they* stuck it out together, married for all those years despite their differences?

look, which, to judge from my father's expression, is not unlike Otto's own. Without so much as nicking Otto's jaw, the trusty lieutenant, whose name is long forgotten, slips the blade under the tightening chinstrap. With a

---

'This looks very familiar,' I said, turning to my father. 'You've got hundreds of photographs of this place, haven't you?'

How many times had I teased my father about his slides of Austria taken over the decades, boxes of them stashed in the attic. Year in, year out, the same places. The buildings change; people turn grey, wrinkle, then disappear altogether; but the lakes and the mountains remain. My mother would nag him to date their photos on the back but he never did. They were simply a record of the fact that he had been there. When was never important.

'He won't sort them out for me,' my mother said, baring her teeth and waving a fist at my father behind his back – her parody of a shrewish wife – muttering 'Old man.'

'There's nothing to stop you,' he said. 'She leaves everything to me, Steve. That's your mother's trouble.'

I had always meant to go up there and sort out the folders of negatives he'd developed himself over thirty years – I remember his makeshift darkroom in the bathroom, the red light, the ticking clock, the smell of the chemicals – but I never did. I wanted both of them to be there, to help with the dates, to tell me who the people were before they were lost for ever. Whenever I sifted through a shoebox full of old photographs, the faces I didn't recognize outnumbered those I did. They were slipping away, mere curiosities, vanishing in front of me for want of a scribble on the back that said who and when they were; their one scrap of immortality worthless for having no name attached.

deft movement of the wrist, he frees his commander not a moment too soon.

'*Vielen* . . . glug . . . *Danke* . . . glug . . .'

By now, the gold medals are weighing heavily on Otto

'Is this the one?' I asked, standing behind a bench, narrowing my eyes to frame the scene in accordance with the famous lakeside picture.

Eager to agree with me, 'Yes,' my mother said. 'This is it.'

'No, no,' my father answered. 'That mountain wasn't there.'

I rolled my eyes and we continued our slow circuit of the lake, as happy as we could ever be. My mother looped her arm round my father's arm or held his hand, the one he would cut between thumb and forefinger in Hari's garden two days later; 'hand in hand with wandring steps and slow'. She sang under her breath, *dee ree-d'Ee dee-o*. . . and, every now and then, I'd call out 'What about this one?' having walked on ahead, unable to keep to my parents' processional pace.

'No.'

I knew in most cases it wasn't the right one, though suggesting every bench on the water's edge as the true location reminded us why we were there, that looking for the place was a reason to be walking, that being together in a beautiful part of the world was, in itself, too awkward to contemplate.

Three-quarters of the way around the lake, my father stopped at the bench the odds told us had to be the one. The shape of the mountains, the distance of the reeds from the edge of the bench, and the angle of the path drifting into the undergrowth agreed with my memory of the photograph.

'This is it, isn't it?' I said, more pleased than my voice was registering.

and they begin dragging him to the bottom. There is only one thing to do. With another flick of the wrist, the lieutenant cuts the medals off and, as they drift languidly to the sea-bed and a watery grave, Otto rises. There is no time to fear the bends as he races to the surface, bursting free with a gasp, water spraying from his shiny pate, his lungs greedily gulping the balmy night air.

'*Mein Gott, mein Gott, mein Gott . . .*'

He is safe.

Bobbing on the surface, he composes himself, casually brushing his handlebar moustache, nodding thanks to his rescuer.

As if to fool us, the local authority had placed a wire bin to one side of the bench, turning it into a Spot the Difference picture.

'It's lovely here,' I said.

Side by side on the bench, my parents smiled shyly for the camera as the shutter clicked.

'It's peaceful, isn't it?' my father said.

'It is,' I replied.

The place had lost none of its charm for my father, the serenity, the clear water, the curve of the mountain range beyond, so, even as my mother teased him, he photographed it again.

'No, really. This *is* incredible!' Then she laughed.

Swapping seats with my father I handed him my camera, put an arm around my mother then smiled into the lens.

'Shall we go to the Lindenallee on the way back?'

'Not now, Fred!' my father groaned, but my mother was eager

[My clean-shaven father had to mime the moustache, which made him look like an angler boasting about a catch.]

In the meantime, Otto's crack team has been swift and efficient, which, in the circumstances, is no more than could be expected but is nevertheless gratifying to their leader, who pretends he is swelling with pride (which he is, though, in the main, he is taking great lungfuls of air).

[My father used to demonstrate just how big he could expand his chest. My heroic father.]

So Otto spies the ships of the Turkish Armada in various stages of submersion and knows his mission is over. Only Otto, his lieutenant and the moonlight watch them sinking, and watch the Turkish sailors swimming shoreward. He has trained his marines well. Even now they are underwater adding further holes to the keels of the stricken vessels, swimming champions every one . . .

[I don't know how much all of this is my father's and how much my own embellishments, added down the years like barnacles on the hapless Turkish ships, but it was

---

for the next stage of our conducted tour, so, with another set of photographs destined to go unmarked, we strolled back the way we had come, Mr and Mrs Schnitzel and their youngest son.

'Perhaps tomorrow,' I said, shaking my head as though I were dismayed, but glad to be there all the same.

one of the first stories, and still a particular favourite, because, when I imagine Otto heading for the Turkish Fleet, I see my father, in Swansea Bay, swimming towards his bride-to-be.

I was usually drifting off by the time he reached the moment where the Turkish Fleet was going under, as good as asleep by the time they reached the bottom. Once, I managed to keep my eyes open until the ceremony for Otto and his heroes, Otto receiving one last gold medal in a banner-decked Bavarian castle. The corridor of saluting soldiers, the fanfares and the drums.

If there ever were tales of Count Otto's retirement years I was never awake to hear them. His voice grown softer and softer, my father would leave the room in slow motion, on tiptoe, holding his breath. I saw him go on one occasion, when he thought sleep had overtaken me and I was past listening. Sunk deep in the pillow, between three-quarters-closed eyelids, I watched him backing out of the room like a courtier, never once turning his back on me, finding the handle by touch. Gently closing the door to leave me in the dark.]

APPENDIX

Lieber Stefan

Here is the Recipe for Wiener Schnitzel using Pork, as you know you must state what Meat you use Wiener Schnitzel is supposed to be Veal.

Pork Steak or loin.
Trim meat neatly, make a few incisions all round the edges.
Beat escallops (Meat Pork Steaks) well.
Have ready three soup plates: one with flour, one with egg mixed with a little cold Milk and a pinch of salt and a third one with white bread crumbs.
Dip Meat first into flour, shake off surplus, then into the beaten egg and finally into the breadcrumbs.
Fry Meat in deep smoking hot oil.
Fry until golden brown on one side. Turn carefully, fry other side.
Drain escallops on kitchen paper and keep hot.
> *A piece of Lemon (essential)*
> *Cranberry sauce not essential*

and as you know I serve the meal with pasta & potatoes, also a few salads made with Kernöl and Wine vinegar.

PS if not clear please ring

> *Love your churlish*

> *Mother*

09/03

2-11-00